Mills & Boon Classics

A chance to read and collect some of the best-loved novels from Mills & Boon – the world's largest publisher of romantic fiction.

Every month, four titles by favourite Mills & Boon authors will be re-published in the *Classics* series.

Lilian Peake

A GIRL ALONE

MILLS & BOON LIMITED
LONDON · TORONTO

First published 1972
Australian copyright 1979
Philippine copyright 1979
Reprinted 1979

© Lilian Peake 1972

ISBN 0 263 73167 7

Set in 10 on 11pt Monotype Plantin

*Made and printed in Great Britain by
C. Nicholls & Company Ltd
The Philips Park Press, Manchester*

CHAPTER I

LORRAINE bent down over the spare bed and tucked in the blankets. 'What I can't understand,' she said to her mother, 'is why we need to take in a paying guest at all.'

Mrs. Ferrers looked a little shocked. 'Oh, we don't *need* to, dear. Now I've got this good job at the employment agency, and with your salary, we're all right.'

Lorraine studied her mother as she drew the candlewick bedspread up and over the blankets. She saw the skill of the hairdresser in her mother's blonde hair, from which all traces of grey had effectively been removed. She saw the eye-shadow and the mascara and the pale pink lipstick. She could not really agree with the way her mother tried to disguise her age, although the make-up she used was delicately applied. It was against her nature to approve of her mother's fight against the inevitable. She wished she would give up the battle and succumb gracefully to middle age like other women.

'I must keep up appearances,' her mother would say, whenever she mentioned it. 'At my age and in my job, I must keep myself looking nice.' She might have added, 'Now I'm a widow, you never know who might come along.'

Lorraine's father had died from heart trouble five years before, and his death had left her mother bewildered and grief-stricken. But before very long she had come to terms with her widowhood and eventually taken up her life again with renewed vigour and with the unfailing optimism which was such an endearing part of her character.

Beryl glanced with distaste at her daughter's brown skirt, shapeless white blouse and old grey cardigan. 'Couldn't you find something better to wear for once, Lorrie? And aren't

7

you going to do your face?' She looked at her watch. 'He'll be here any minute.'

Lorraine frowned. 'You know I never "do" my face, Mum. So why should I bother for him? And no, I'm not going to change.' She looked down at her clothes and knew her mother wouldn't be seen dead in them. She had said so more than once.

'And you're such a nice shape, too, dear. You should show it off, not hide it underneath all that bagginess. The trouble is, you've got your father's primness, dear man that he was. You're all stiff and starchy. You want to break out a bit, Lorrie. It shows, dear, it shows in your face.' She re-arranged the flowers on the small dining-table—they had made the bedroom into a pleasant bed-sitter—and said, with her back to her daughter, 'The way you talk, you make it sound as though Alan's not welcome.'

'As far as I'm concerned, he isn't. You know what I think of journalists.'

'But he's different, Lorrie. He's Nancy Darby's boy. When she wrote and told me Alan was coming to work on the local evening paper, I—well, I thought about this room standing empty and——'

'And you offered it to him.'

'Only for a little while, dear,' Beryl said, trying to placate her daugher, perhaps falsely so, because she knew that she personally would do her best to make her old friend's son stay as long as possible. 'Only till he finds something more suitable.' She paused and drifted remini-scently back to the past. 'I remember seeing him when he was a little lad, a bit quiet, with nothing much to say for himself.' She hesitated, then went on, 'The last time I saw Nancy, and that was a few years ago, she told me he'd changed a lot.'

'Is he married?'

'No, although you'd think he would be at his age. He must be in his middle thirties, Nancy did say he was one for the girls now.' She laughed self-consciously, as if she were a girl herself. Lorraine thought, 'Well, if someone didn't know how old she was, they'd never guess.' She began to suspect that her mother was actually looking forward to the paying guest's arrival.

The doorbell rang. Beryl Ferrers' hand jerked to her hair. 'That's him, dear. Let him in, Lorrie. I must tidy myself.'

Lorraine went down the stairs slowly, conscious for some odd reason of her total lack of make-up and her general dowdiness. Now she wished she had taken her mother's advice and changed. Now, when it was too late, something inside her wanted to impress this man whose outline she could see through the patterned glass of the front door. Then she told herself not to be a fool. 'He's just a journalist,' she reflected, 'the scum of the earth.' And with that rebellious thought gleaming in her eyes, she opened the door.

The man on the doorstep saw her face raised mutinously to his. He listened to the mumbled and wholly insincere welcome and waited to be invited in. The invitation was so long in coming that he had time to size up—and down—the girl who stood on the threshold, barring his way. His eyes did a swift analytical job on her. They took her apart, assessed her and put her together again, in the space of a few seconds. As she stood back at last to let him in, she wondered precisely what was the result of that bit of research. She had to wait a long time before she knew the answer.

She told him, her face stiff with dislike, her eyes challenging his, her voice edgy and grating, 'I'll show you upstairs to your room, Mr. Darby. Will you please follow me?'

As she climbed the stairs with the tall, dark-haired man behind her, she wished more than ever that she had at least changed out of her laddered stockings and worn her sandals instead of her old lace-up shoes.

On the landing her mother pounced and took over. Lorraine heard the warm and spontaneous greeting, heard it returned in pleasant, precise tones, saw the gripping hand-shake and exchange of smiles and left them.

She could not join in the general rejoicing. She would not change her opinion of journalists simply because this one was the son of an old friend of her mother's. They were all the same, she told herself, desperately trying to justify her deep and almost obsessive dislike of the 'breed' as she called them. They were shiftless, heavy-drinking rabble, devoid of morals and completely insensitive to the feelings of others.

And this man, in spite of his good looks and proud bearing, was no different. In fact, she toyed gloatingly with the thought, because it added justification to her mistrust of the man, all those assets probably made him worse than others of his kind. 'One for the girls' indeed! She remembered the expression in his eyes as he had summed her up even before setting foot in the house. She drew in her lips angrily as she thought of the dismissal which was contained in his glance, almost as if he had mentally lifted her up and put her out of the way. He had trampled on her with his eyes, she told herself furiously as she went downstairs to set the table. And she, Lorraine Ferrers, teacher of English at Walkley School for Girls, was not going to be treated as an irritating obstacle to be removed from anybody's path, let alone a journalist's.

As she spread the cloth over the table, she heard her mother's voice on the landing. 'You *must* have a meal with us this evening, Alan, but after today, of course, you'll probably prefer to eat in your own room.'

'Thank goodness for that,' Lorraine thought, as she arranged place-settings for three. Her mother came down and helped her prepare the salad and slice the cold ham.

'He's such a nice boy, dear,' she was saying. Lorraine smiled grimly, knowing her mother could see only the good in everyone she met. 'I do hope you'll get on well with him. Make the effort, Lorrie, for my sake.'

Lorraine shook her head with decision. She loved her mother, but—make the effort? That she could not, would not do, even for her.

Beryl looked at her daughter and put her head on one side as though she were coaxing a difficult child. 'Lorrie, go and do your face. Please, dear, for my sake.'

Lorraine shrugged. That, she supposed, was something she could do to please her, without going against any of her principles. She trod quietly up the stairs, tip-toeing past the spare bedroom, went into her own room and closed the door.

She combed her hair, and tied it back again with the small piece of black ribbon. She applied a layer of powder. Lipstick? No, she drew the line at that. She refused to waste her lipstick on Mr. Alan Darby. She turned her back resolutely on the dowdy girl in the mirror and went downstairs.

The paying guest was standing, hands in pockets, looking uncomfortable. He turned as Lorraine appeared at the dining-room door. His raised eyebrows greeted her stony glance.

'There's no need to wait in here, Mr. Darby. There are some comfortable armchairs in the sitting-room.'

'I'm perfectly happy, Miss Ferrers. I've been sitting too long in the train.'

'You've come from London, Mr. Darby?'

'I have, Miss Ferrers.'

Lorraine looked at him, suspecting by his tone that he was mocking her deliberate formality. Mrs. Ferrers hurried in with a jug of milk which she put on the table. 'My goodness me,' she said, 'don't be so formal, you two. You know he's Alan, Lorrie. Call him that, dear, not Mr. Darby.' She shook momentarily with distaste. 'And Alan, this is Lorrie. Lorraine, really,' she smiled fondly at her daughter, 'but

Lorrie's my own special name for her.'

Alan bowed to Lorraine very slightly, and she turned away from the amusement in his eyes.

'I only call my friends by their first names,' Lorraine threw at her mother as she went into the kitchen.

Mrs. Ferrers, shocked, stumbled over words as she tried to compensate for her daughter's rudeness. 'She doesn't mean it, you know,' Lorraine heard her say. 'Take no notice, Alan.'

Lorraine switched on the kettle and made the tea.

'Ah now,' her mother bustled about as she took the teapot from Lorraine's hands, 'put the cosy on it, Lorrie. Sit down, Alan. Here, opposite Lorrie. Lorrie, pour the tea, there's a dear.'

Lorraine managed to avoid Alan Darby's eyes for most of the meal, but later, as they drank their tea, having nowhere else to look, she found her eyes wandering to him. She noticed that his hair was so dark it was almost black. She saw how his nostrils widened slightly at the end of his long straight nose and that his jawline was square and obstinate. He started on a cigarette and, to her discomfiture, openly contemplated her face through the smoke, with those searching, take-apart eyes of his. She straightened her features into a mask, giving him little to go on as he silently sorted through her hidden virtues and obvious shortcomings.

Beryl Ferrers was talking to Alan about his job. There was a break in the conversation and Lorraine smiled slightly and threw at him across the table, 'We'll have to guard our tongues from now on, I suppose.' She waited for the eyebrows to rise. They did.

'Having a journalist in the house,' she mused, as if talking to herself, 'is a bit like being "bugged"—having a hidden microphone buried in the flower vase, or under the carpet. Like,' she went on, anticipating with relish the reaction of the man opposite, 'having a spy in the family.'

She knew she had drawn blood by the minor explosion which erupted momentarily in those keen grey eyes. But she had to admire the skilful way he hid his annoyance. It was only his eyes that gave away his feelings. They blazed for an instant like a smouldering fire which had had petrol thrown on it. Then all was as still as before. The eyes narrowed until they could hardly be seen.

'Miss Ferrers, of course, has known many journalists in her time.'

'Journalists?' Beryl looked at her daughter. 'You've never known any journalists, have you, Lorrie?'

'No—er—no, I haven't exactly—known—any.' She flushed at the gleam in those eyes. 'Thank goodness,' she added with a smile. 'No, my acquaintance has merely been through their works, the rubbish they fill the papers with.' She settled back in her chair and met those eyes squarely. 'I spend most of my days, Mr. Darby, trying to undo the damage which newspapermen do to the English of school-children.'

She warmed to her subject, feeling not in the least chilled by the frost in the face of the man she was addressing. 'The journalistic garbage which people imbibe every day with their morning papers is so toxic that it eats at the roots of the English language like dental decay.'

Her mother gasped. 'Lorrie! How can you say such things!' She looked at Alan, appealing for his forgiveness. 'Take no notice of her, Alan. She's a teacher, you see,' as if that explained all her daughter's faults and waywardness. 'She teaches English at the girls' school in the town.' She whispered behind her hand, 'Between you and me, it's a bit old-fashioned and stuffy. Needs some new blood, especially at the top. Time that headmistress retired, she's making all the teachers like herself.'

'I doubt,' said Alan Darby, looking pointedly at Lorraine, 'if the new blood is needed only at the top.' He rested his elbows on the table and eyed her with distaste. 'It seems to me, Miss Ferrers, that your approach to the whole subject is much too fastidious and narrow. I might tell you that the majority of people, and I mean the majority, like reading that "journalistic garbage", as you call it.' He smiled slightly as he tapped ash into the ash-tray. 'If I may say so, that very expression smacks of the "journalese" you so despise.' He seemed to enjoy seeing the girl opposite him squirm uncomfortably in her seat.

'Don't judge others by your own rather snobbish standards,' he went on with a flick of contempt in his eyes. 'We journalists have to cater for the rest of the world, not just the likes of you, with your superior mentality. Open your eyes, Miss Ferrers, look around and you'll see that there are many ordinary people with ordinary intellect who want to read about everyday things in everyday words.'

Lorraine flushed. 'It's obvious,' she spat out, 'we don't speak the same *language*, Mr. Darby, so——'

He cut in, disregarding her bad-tempered outburst, 'Where English is concerned, you can't shut yourself away in an ivory tower and turn your back on the changes that are taking place around you. I'm horrified that you, as a teacher, should even try to do so. You can't keep on for ever speaking and writing in the stilted formal language of the past.'

For some reason Lorraine could not comprehend, his criticism stung her beyond endurance. She started to clear away the dishes. 'This discussion is pointless. I'll tell you here and now,' she raised her voice as though she were about to make an earth-shattering pronouncement, 'I regard journalists as the highest-paid *unskilled* workers in the country. I rate their job as being even less important than road-sweeping. That at least clears away the rubbish and doesn't create it!'

She swept from the stunned silence into the kitchen, but somehow she couldn't take much pleasure from her Pyrrhic victory. She had an odd feeling that she had hurt herself as

14

much as she had hurt her enemy.

Lorraine and her mother usually got up late on Sundays, but that weekend they both rose early. They had yet to learn the habits of their paying guest and until they did, decided to feel their way. Lorraine cooked his breakfast and took it up on a tray. She stood on the landing and waited for him to answer her knock. He was up and dressed and let her in with a brief smile. She put the tray on the table.

'I have a message for you from my mother,' she said, talking like a child who had learned the lesson by heart and was now repeating it parrot-fashion. 'She insists that you must have everything you want and that you mustn't hesitate to ask for something if there's anything missing.'

He gave her an odd look and she caught the corner of a smile as he turned his head away. 'I see. And are you going to act as my waitress, my provider of all that I need?' She began to suspect the seriousness of his expression. Those take-apart eyes had turned towards her and were at work again. 'Because if so,' he contemplated her old grey stretch slacks and loose-hanging blouse, 'I shall need a secretary, full-time, of course; a fact-finder to do background research for me and someone to answer the telephone. Then there are all the humdrum housewifely jobs such as sewer-on of buttons, someone to keep me tidy, do my washing . . .' his voice tailed off, 'er—and so on. Among other things,' he added with a gleam in his eyes. 'Odd,' he smiled with mock surprise, 'I've almost talked myself into taking a wife,' his sideways glance was intended to provoke, 'a thing no man in his right mind should ever do.'

Lorraine knew she was expected to smile, so she did, but it was a tight-lipped affair. His expression closed down and she knew he had written her off as a hopeless case.

'Thank you for cooking my breakfast,' he said, turning away, and somehow she felt like a schoolchild being dismissed from the classroom.

15

The morning passed quietly and she gathered her wits and her notes for school, and tried to get herself into the right frame of mind to tackle a new term.

'What time is Hugh coming?' Beryl asked when they were washing the lunch dishes.

'Oh, the usual. Threeish.'

'Going out?'

'Doubt it. I feel lazy, probably reacting in advance to the start of a new session at school. I always hate the first day of the autumn term. So much fuss over details.'

For Hugh she combed her hair, then pulled it back tightly from her face and retied the ribbon. She changed into a skirt and clean white blouse and put on lipstick to bring a touch of colour to her face. She peered at her reflection and for the first time was vaguely dissatisfied.

There was something missing—no animation, that was it, no life, no charm. Her mother was right, she told herself. Her primness did show in her face. And she knew that all the cosmetics in the world could not make up for what was lacking inside her. She ought to be feeling happy that Hugh was coming. Her eyes should be shining, cheeks glowing, senses heightened. She thought about Hugh, fair-haired, stolid, pleasant-looking and comforting. She knew then why her pulses never wavered from their steady beat even when he kissed her, which was not often.

Alan was in the kitchen, talking. He smiled as Lorraine passed him, as if offering a peace token, but she didn't smile back. 'When Hugh comes,' she told her mother, 'we'll sit in the garden.'

Beryl nodded and explained to Alan, 'Hugh's Lorraine's boy-friend. He's a teacher at the same school.'

Alan asked Lorraine, smiling and still trying to improve relations between them, 'Does he teach English, too, and share your dislike of me and my kind?'

'No,' Lorraine answered, looking at him sourly. 'Chemistry's his line.'

16

'Ah, then I'm probably not such a villain in his eyes as I am in yours, with your puritanical approach to your own subject.' He leaned back against the kitchen table and smiled irritatingly. 'Very respectable profession, teaching. Unexciting, dull, routine and at times, soul-destroying. In the end, teachers become like their occupation, dull and too respectable for words.'

Lorraine swung round to face him. She didn't like it now he had turned on her those weapons of attack and provocation which she had used on him. 'Better to be those things, Mr. Darby, then downright lying sensationalists like you and your—your brethren. Anyway, what do you know about teachers?'

'I can only go by those I've met, and in my job I've come across quite a few. And I'm talking to one now, aren't I? I see no reason to alter my opinion of them even—or perhaps I should say especially—after meeting you.'

It was a statement which was plainly meant to incite her to anger, and it succeeded, but she held it in, although some of it must have seeped through into her eyes because her mother said, 'Now calm down, Lorrie, he's only teasing, aren't you, Alan?'

That smile grew to maddening proportions as he left them and returned to his room.

Beryl chided her daughter, 'You really shouldn't speak to him like that, dear. He's our guest, after all.'

'Paying,' she put in nastily, but her mother went on, 'And he's really such a nice boy.'

'Boy?' she snorted. '*Boy?*' There was nothing boyish about that man, with his too-knowing eyes and his deliberately cynical approach to everything.

'Yes, dear,' her mother went on mildly, 'once you get over his funny ways and get through to him, he's a nice boy. I told you before, he was a quiet lad when he was younger.'

Lorraine shrugged. She went outside to get the folding chairs from the shed and placed them on the lawn facing the sun. She was sitting in one of them when Hugh came. He bent down and kissed her on the cheek.

'Hallo, Lorraine.' He lowered himself into the chair beside her. 'Just met your paying guest. He was going to post a letter as I was coming in. Nice chap he seems. We chatted for a few minutes.'

'You chatted? What about?'

'Oh, this and that. Surprising how much ground you can cover with some people in the space of a few minutes.'

'I don't like him.'

Hugh was surprised. 'I can't see anything about him to dislike. Intelligent too—for a journalist.'

Lorraine responded at once. 'I do see what you mean,' she said, eager to be on the attack and justify her strong feelings on the subject—so strong in this case that they even surprised her. 'They're confidence tricksters. They're like scavengers. They're always looking for trouble. They feed on the refuse of other people's lives. They dig up every-thing that should be decently buried.'

Lorraine could see Hugh was trying to stop her, so she followed his eyes and jerked round to see Alan standing behind her. Her heart bumped guiltily, and she tried to read his expression. She couldn't. He was holding out her knitting.

'Your mother said you wanted this.'

'Thank you.' She hoped she sounded cooler than she felt. But she could not understand her embarrassment, as until that moment, she had felt no qualms at all about hurting him. In fact, she had wanted to keep on hurting him and never stop.

Hugh jumped up. 'Sit down, Alan,' he indicated his chair. 'I'll get myself another.'

'Good heavens, no, Hugh, thanks all the same. Wouldn't dream of interrupting such a cosy, domestic sort of tête-à-tête.'

His smile held a touch of derision and Lorraine scowled

18

as he walked away.

'Alan? Hugh? First names already?' she asked.

'Why not? He suggested it.'

Lorraine experienced a ridiculous stab of jealousy over-laid with a curious sense of regret at having rejected the chance to call Alan by his first name like everyone else.

That night, when Lorraine went up to bed, Alan and her mother were on the landing. 'So you were actually in Fleet Street?' Beryl was asking in tones of awe, as Lorraine passed them on the way to her bedroom.

'I was.' He named a well-known national newspaper. 'As a sub-editor.'

'So this new job will be a big change?'

'It will. A pleasant one, too, I hope, without the stresses and strains involved in working in Fleet Street.'

'And what will you be? A sub-editor again?'

'No. News editor, so this job represents promotion. I'll have to feel my way from the big stuff on the national level to the big-town type of gossip.'

Lorraine couldn't resist joining in as she stood at the bathroom door in her housecoat. 'You sound very conde-scending, Mr. Darby. How, I wonder, could you lower yourself to come *down* to this level? Why did you leave Fleet Street? Couldn't you make the grade?'

He flushed with anger. 'No doubt you will choose not to believe me, Miss Ferrers, but I couldn't stand the rat race.'

Lorraine smiled patronisingly. 'I *quite* understand.'

He tightened up at her tone of voice. The look he gave her made her whole body tingle as she remembered with a shock that her housecoat was semi-transparent and that the clothing she was wearing underneath could hardly be de-scribed as adequate. She dived into the bathroom and told herself that her cheeks were hot with the steam rising from the bath-water.

They were still talking when she came out of the bathroom twenty minutes later. She called goodnight to them both, but only her mother answered.

Lorraine had to go up through her mental gears and force herself into top speed for the new term. After the summer vacation, it was never easy to get into the right frame of mind and this term it seemed harder than ever. There were other things on her mind, one of them being the continuing and more than irritating presence of her mother's paying guest.

She managed to put him out of her thoughts as she walked into the school, but not for long. The first words that her friend Ann greeted her with in the corridor just after assembly were, 'I hear you've got a lodger.'

Lorraine pretended to wince at her workmanlike description of the paying guest. 'Don't call him that, Ann. He's top quality, didn't you know?'

Hugh, who was standing beside her, said, 'I don't know why Lorraine is so sarcastic about him. I've met him and I can't see what there is to hold against him.'

'I dislike him on principle. But it's not only that. He's overbearing and—and rude, and thinks far too much of himself.'

'Now you make me more eager than ever to meet him,' Ann declared, smoothing her lank, too-short hair and whipping off her brown-rimmed glasses. 'I may be getting a bit long in the tooth—older than he is, probably, but these days, with a bit of clever plastic surgery, what does that matter?'

They laughed and Hugh said, 'I think Lorraine must bring out the worst in him.'

'Thanks for the tip, Hugh,' Ann replaced her glasses. 'When—and if—I meet the man, I'll remember to butter him up as only I can. Anyway, Hugh, it doesn't sound as though you need worry. I doubt if you've got a rival there.'

20

Hugh laughed shortly. 'No. Pleasant though the man is——'

Lorraine started to protest, but Ann said, 'Now now...'

Hugh went on, 'He's definitely not Lorraine's type, nor,' he looked at her thoughtfully, 'would she be his.'

Lorraine felt absurdly annoyed. 'Why, what's wrong with me?'

'As far as I'm concerned,' Hugh answered slowly, 'not very much.'

'Not very much?' Lorraine felt bewildered, because the answer should have been 'nothing'. It implied that even Hugh—solid, dependable, undemanding Hugh—thought there was something wrong with her.

'Alan Darby would want something much more—sophisticated,' Hugh persisted, 'more—more...' He sought for the right word. Lorraine supplied it.

'Polished?'

Hugh nodded and Ann saw Lorraine start to bristle. She intervened quickly, 'Now we're skating over slippery ground, where anything could happen. So let's veer off it fast before tempers rise.'

'Time for my class, anyway.' Hugh left them and Lorraine and Ann parted.

All through the day, as Lorraine taught one group of schoolgirls after another—girls in all stages of development, from the younger ones who giggled and whispered, to the sixth-formers who, to her relief, were more serious and intelligently alert—she thought about Hugh's remark and it rankled badly.

'Stiff and starchy,' her mother had said. 'Your primness shows, dear, it shows in your face.'

That evening at home she stared into her dressing-table mirror. For the first time ever, she badly wanted to do something about it. 'Twenty-six years old and looking all my years and more,' she thought with dismay, staring at her unmade-up face and tugged-back dark brown hair.

21

She studied her features in detail. Firmly arched eyebrows, not a badly shaped nose, reasonably good mouth. And her eyes? Blue with long curling lashes. Spoilt, though, by a withdrawn and lonely look.

Her mother and Alan were out. She went into her mother's bedroom and picked up her cosmetics one by one. After a few minutes, she congratulated herself on having used them with commendable skill for a novice.

The startling result of her efforts made her look at the clothes she was wearing. They hardly went with her new image. Tomorrow, she promised herself, swiftly counting up her money, she would go after school to the shops and bring her wardrobe up to date.

It was Hugh's remark, she told herself, which had made her come to such a decision. It had nothing whatever to do with the man now living in their house.

Her mother came in unexpectedly early and caught her on the landing. 'Lorrie, my dear, you look marvellous! Your face—you've borrowed my things?'

'You don't mind, Mum?'

'Mind? Dear, I'm delighted. Where's Alan?' She tapped on his door.

'He's out.'

'What a pity. I'd have liked him to see you like that. He was only saying the other day . . .'

'I'll wipe this stuff off.' Lorraine didn't wait to hear Alan Darby's disparaging remarks.

Her mother turned on her coaxing tone. 'Leave it on, dear, at least till he gets home.'

Ignoring her mother's plea, Lorraine went purposefully into the bathroom.

'Oh, all right,' her mother gave in, 'but you can always borrow my stuff any time you want, Lorrie.'

Alan came home after Lorraine had gone to bed. She heard him talking on the landing. Her mother asked him how he liked his new job.

'Fine,' he answered. 'I feel stimulated instead of half dead as I used to at the end of the day.'

'Lorrie's in bed,' she heard her mother say. Then she lowered her voice and Lorraine knew Alan was being told about her session with the cosmetics. 'How could she let me down like that?' Lorraine fumed, almost in tears, 'treating me like a child.' She heard Alan laugh and gripped her pillow in two soft bulging handfuls. Never again, she swore, would she put on a speck of make-up, not even lipstick. She had to get even somehow with Mr. Alan Darby.

Nevertheless, the next time Hugh called, she borrowed her mother's cosmetics. She put on a new pair of blue stretch slacks and a pink sleeveless blouse and she had to acknowledge that there was a decided improvement in her appearance. When she joined Hugh in the lounge, his head jerked back and he looked at her as though he had never seen her before.

'You're different,' he said. 'What have you done?'

'Nothing,' she answered carelessly and turned away from his stare. She felt embarrassed, encumbered by his interest. Now she had made him notice her, she wished she hadn't. But if she had not done it for him, then who else——? Impatiently she grabbed her knitting and dropped into an armchair.

'Did I tell you,' Hugh said, opening the newspaper and sitting on the couch, 'that I met Alan in the town after school yesterday? We had a cup of tea together and I discovered he's got a transistor radio to sell.'

'He's out,' she said shortly. 'He's out almost every evening. I haven't seen him for days.'

'Never mind. If he comes in before I go, I'll have a quick look at it then. I've been wanting one for months, and he's asking quite a reasonable price.'

During the evening, Lorraine made some tea, then continued with her knitting. Most of her dates with Hugh were spent like this, all of them uneventful and dull. She had never questioned it before, but now that Hugh was apparently beginning to regard her as something more than just an extension of the armchair she was occupying, she began to realise how much was missing from their relationship. All the same, every time she caught him looking at her, she wished perversely that he wouldn't.

Hugh lifted his head and listened as the front door opened and closed.

'It's only my mother,' Lorraine told him, but he got up and went into the hall.

'Hallo, Alan,' he said, 'nice to see you. Come in.'

How could Hugh invite him in, Lorraine thought angrily, without asking her first?

Alan stood in the doorway and although Lorraine kept on knitting, she knew his eyes were on her. At last she looked up and caught his sardonic expression. She knitted again furiously. Well, what had she expected? Admiration?

'I must surely be interrupting——' There it was again, the mockery, the half-hidden amusement.

'Lorraine,' Hugh indicated the teapot, 'would there be ... ?'

She put down her knitting and stood up. 'I'll get a cup and saucer.' She looked at Alan and hoped her look froze him. 'Sit down, Mr. Darby. Make yourself comfortable.'

'You're very kind,' he said, with malice in his smile. His eyes did a speedy piece of research all over her. When she returned and poured out his tea, he was reclining on the couch next to Hugh and they were talking.

Lorraine handed him his cup. 'Sugar, Mr. Darby?'

He smiled his baiting smile and said, 'Oh, please, lots of it. The more the better.' Lorraine knew he was not referring to the white crystals in the sugar basin.

Her restless fingers clamped on to the knitting needles and she did her best to look relaxed and unconcerned. Those probing, analytical eyes wandered from her to Hugh and back again and a questioning shadow flickered and

24

faded as he turned to Hugh and said, 'So your subject's chemistry. How do you like teaching?'

Hugh shrugged. 'I'd like it better if it were a mixed school. Concentrated "girl" gets a bit much at times.'

Alan laughed, 'Now that's something I'd never complain about!'

Lorraine thought of her mother's remark, 'He's one for the girls.' She made a mistake in her knitting and tutted madly, which brought Alan's attention back to her.

'And you, Miss Ferrers, you've taken to teaching like a duck to water?'

'I chose my career, Mr. Darby. It wasn't forced on me. I like the routine, the regularity . . .'

He nodded. 'The well-ordered existence, the dull, stolid unexciting approach to life of your colleagues, the pages of notes from which you never deviate, the unimaginative presentation of your subject which it never occurs to you to vary. Row on row of bright kids, full of potential, all being conditioned to accept what they're being taught without question.'

She flared. He had turned the tables on her. He was employing her tactics of direct positive attack so effectively she felt she could have stuffed her knitting into his mouth until he choked, just to stop him talking.

'What do you know of a teacher's life?' she challenged, thoroughly aroused. 'We teach children things we know to be true and accurate and which will be of use to them in later life. *We* don't search in life's dustbins and bring out putrefying matter and force it down people's throats like you do.'

His smile was slow and without warmth. His cold eyes appraised her flushed cheeks and over-bright eyes. 'Your criticisms are, as usual, emotional and destructive. Like many people, you've allowed your opinions to be shaped almost entirely by prejudice and ignorance.'

He went on, not allowing her to interrupt, although she

tried, 'Your attitude to the press is not uncommon. But what you, as a teacher of English, should know is that reporting is not merely writing. It's highly specialised. It's the seeking out of portents, signposts to the future, in present-day events. It's up to the journalist, with his so-called "nose for news", to discover such secrets, and if necessary, draw attention to them.'

'What you're trying to say,' Hugh said in his slow fashion, 'is—seeing tomorrow in today.'

'Now that,' said Alan, drawing a pen from his pocket and scribbling on a piece of paper, 'sums up very nicely what I mean.'

'I don't care if you are convincing Hugh, you'll never convince me,' Lorraine declared, annoyed with Hugh for joining the enemy. 'Reporters are always searching for "angles" and over-emphasising trivialities, and this has the effect of distorting so-called "news" out of all proportion to its real importance. In other words, they're out to fool the public.'

Alan shook his head pityingly. 'I'm sorry for the kids at your school. It's quite unfair to give them such a biased, misinformed teacher.'

Hugh laughed, trying to ease the tension. 'If you're not careful, Alan, she'll be throwing something at you.'

'What, Miss Ferrers lose control sufficiently to behave like a normal, uninhibited human being? Never!'

Hugh laughed again, but it was an uncomfortable sound. 'My my, you two do love each other! And on such short acquaintance, too. Let's change the subject before you both declare open warfare. About that transistor radio, Alan ...'

'Yes, of course, Hugh. It's in my room. Come and have a look at it.'

Hugh followed him quickly to the door, almost as though he were eager to be out of the hostile atmosphere. 'Be back soon,' he called over his shoulder.

They went upstairs, still talking. Lorraine stayed in her

chair, beside herself with fury. She knew that if she had not been furious, she would have cried, and that would have been ridiculous.

Hugh did not come down again until it was time for him to leave. Lorraine went into the hall and noticed Alan halfway down the stairs. Hugh raised his right hand and said goodbye to him. In his other hand he held a transistor radio with loving care. He kissed Lorraine's cheek absent-mindedly. She had the feeling that if he had been called upon to kiss the radio, he would have done it with far more feeling.

She closed the front door and heard Alan call softly, 'Lorraine?'

She stopped in her tracks at the sound of her name. He came down to the hall.

'I'm a peace-loving creature. I hate war, especially within a family.' He held out his hand. 'Shall we call a cease-fire?'

Family? How dared he insinuate that he was a member of this family! Lorraine ignored his hand. 'Goodnight, Mr. Darby.' She walked away.

He took a short, sharp breath and strode up the stairs without another word.

CHAPTER II

LORRAINE and Alan ignored each other after that. Even if she had smiled at him, which she had no intention of doing, she felt he would have pretended she wasn't there. At least, she told herself, they couldn't quarrel if they didn't even speak.

She returned to her old ways of dressing and tied her hair back more tightly than ever. She had arranged to go for a walk with Ann one Saturday afternoon. Ann arrived dressed in her oldest clothes and Lorraine wore her old slacks and an anorak that had seen better days.

'Where's this lodger you keep grumbling about?'

'Sh-sh, paying guest, Ann dear, not lodger! It's a good thing my mother's in the garden and can't hear you. Anyway, he regards himself as one of the family now, and so does Mum. She natters to him every time she sees him. Sometimes she has a cup of tea with him, sometimes he comes down here. When he does, I go up to my room until he's gone.'

'My word, he must be a ghastly type if that's the effect he has on you. I gather he's out, since you're speaking so frankly about him?'

'He is out, as usual. When he's not, he spends the rest of the time in his room. Or on the phone.'

'Any—er—feminine appendages, any women in his life?'

Lorraine shrugged and struggled with a tight feeling inside her. 'Dozens, probably. Shall we go?'

Lorraine called to her mother that they were leaving. She was half asleep in a garden chair and making the most of the unbelievably fine spell of September weather. Ann waved to her and they went out.

The bus stop was only a few minutes' walk away and the

bus took them as far as the entrance to a semi-cultivated park on the outskirts of the town. The deep green turf gave softly under their feet and they wandered between the trees and climbed the hill to gaze at the view.

Lorraine experienced again the buoyant feeling, a lift of the spirits which that hilltop always gave her. Standing there, eyes sweeping the landscape for many miles around, she felt a sense of peace which for some curious reason she badly needed.

She looked below at the people climbing up and looked again. She frowned and caught her breath. One figure stood out. Tall, dark-haired, hands in pockets, head slightly bent in effort, came a man striding slowly, purposefully upwards.

'There he is,' Lorraine said urgently, her finger pointing from inside her anorak pocket. 'There's your man.'

'My man? Tell me where, quick, before he passes me by for ever.'

'He's coming up the hill.' Lorraine looked round, stiff with fright, seeking cover. 'Can't I hide somewhere?'

Ann looked at her queerly. 'Why do you want to hide? Is he dangerous or something?'

He was too near now to take evasive action. He had seen them. What would he do? Lorraine wondered feverishly. Nod and go on his way? Ignore them or stand and talk? She saw the flash of recognition in his eyes. She willed him to go past, but obviously her will-power was too weak. He stopped. 'Good afternoon, Miss Ferrers.'

It was the first time he had spoken to her for days. She nodded, avoiding his eyes. She introduced him to Ann, clumsily, reluctantly.

'Ann, this is—er—our pay—our guest, Alan Darby. He's staying with us.' She stopped, thoroughly confused by the amusement in his eyes, then realised she hadn't finished. 'Er—Mr. Darby, this is Ann Palmer, a friend of mine.'

As they shook hands, Ann raised quick astonished eyebrows. Then she smiled. 'So you're Mr. Darby? I understand you're a journalist.'

'I am.' He glanced at Lorraine, a smile hovering. 'Do I take cover?'

'Why?'

'Don't tell me you can't see my cloven hoof, not to mention my horns?' Lorraine hated the smile which creased his face. 'I'm sure Miss Ferrers hasn't minced her words when she has talked about me. She hardly spares me to my face, so I can't believe she is less uncharitable behind my back.'

Lorraine forced herself to smile sweetly. She knew it would give effect to the tartness of her words. 'What makes you so sure I even think about you, Mr. Darby, let alone talk about you?'

He pretended to shiver. 'I asked for that!'

Ann was plainly charmed by him. They strolled along the ridge, Alan between them, and he was saying, 'You're a teacher, too, Miss Palmer?'

'Yes, I'm one of Them. Unfortunately, I've been in the game so long, I've grown like Them.' She looked at Lorraine. 'So watch out, Lorraine. Make your stay in the profession as short as possible. It sort of seeps into your bones. Someone called it "the touch of the chalk". Once you get it, it seems to leave its mark for ever.'

'I've got it already,' Lorraine said carelessly. 'Ask Mr. Darby. I'm—how did he put it?—dull, humdrum and too respectable for words.'

'You have a good memory, Miss Ferrers,' the man beside her said softly.

'When things rankle, Mr. Darby, they tend to stick.' Then she realised just how much she had given away. Dismayed, she looked up to see if he had noticed. He had. Victory flooded his eyes for a split second, then died away like a light being switched on and off in a dark room. She felt she hated him more than ever.

By the time Lorraine had recovered her balance, he was chatting to Ann about modern art. 'I've got press tickets for the opening of an art exhibition in the town. I was thinking of going alone, but I'd be delighted if you would come with me.'

Ann glanced quickly at Lorraine, but her hesitation was so slight it passed unnoticed. 'You know, I'd love to, Mr. Darby. Are you sure there's no one else you'd rather take? Lorraine, for instance?'

He glanced distastefully at Lorraine and she flushed. 'Good heavens, no. I don't want to be quarrelling all the evening. No, there's no one else I'd rather take, I assure you.'

So they discussed a time to meet. 'I'll take you to a meal. Would you like that?'

Ann stopped in her tracks. 'But—but it really doesn't matter . . .'

He was not listening. He was running through the names of possible eating places and mentioned one as being especially good. He suggested a time and Ann agreed, thanking him profusely.

'Not at all. I'm sure I shall enjoy your company.'

He went on his way without a backward glance at Lorraine, and Ann turned large eyes to her. 'You little so-and-so, keeping him under your hat! What do you mean by telling me all those lies about him? He's a dish, dear. He's swept me off my feet. Me, at my advanced age, and with me spectacles an' all!'

'You're only thirty-three, Ann. Younger than he is—he's thirty-six, if you want to know.'

'When you think of all the fabulous females he must have in tow—and he asked me out! This calls for a new dress.'

The tight knot inside Lorraine was there again and nothing she could do would untie it this time. 'I mustn't be jealous,' she told herself, 'because that would mean I cared, and of course I don't care a damn for that man.'

She could not enjoy the rest of the walk. She found herself straining her eyes for a sight of his tall figure and

31

called herself a fool. She knew she should be glad he had gone, and had not encumbered them with his presence for the rest of the afternoon.

While her mother cooked the Sunday lunch, Lorraine spread her folders and papers over the dining-room table and prepared notes for the class she took at the local technical college every Monday evening. She had been doing it for the past two years and found the extra money it brought in very useful. She enjoyed it too, liking the more liberal atmosphere of the college. It was a pleasant change from the cloistered, shut-in feeling the school gave her sometimes. She liked the students, who got down to work willingly and without first being chided and pushed by the teacher.

Alan usually had his lunch in his room, but it seemed that this time he was having it with them. Lorraine heard her mother invite him to join them and he accepted in a pleased sort of voice.

Lorraine served the meal while her mother did the talking. Beryl was rarely lost for words and for once Lorraine was glad. Her mother turned to her.

'Did I tell you, dear, that James is taking me for a run this afternoon?'

James Cornish was Beryl's employer. He was a widower and they seemed to be on friendly terms these days. Somehow the idea upset Lorraine, although she knew it should have made her glad. 'Everyone's got someone,' she thought childishly. 'Even Ann now. But I've got Hugh, haven't I?'

'Are you going out, Alan?' Beryl was asking.

'Probably. There's someone I want to see who's only in at weekends.'

Lorraine forestalled her mother's question. 'It's a lovely day, so I'll sit in the garden and do nothing.'

'A lazy afternoon, Miss Ferrers?'

'Yes.' She frowned. 'Dull, ordinary, unexciting—and

32

very respectable, like me.' She knew she sounded sulky, but that was how she felt. She could almost hear his smile, and ground her teeth inside closed lips.

She heard Alan leave the house soon after lunch and while her mother was changing, Lorraine took out the two-piece swimsuit she had bought for her holiday with Ann in the Scilly Isles. She had never dared to wear it either before or since, because it was brief, a brilliant red and, to her, a little too eye-catching. She looked at it for a long time, trying to make up her mind. She glanced outside at the warm, inviting sunshine and came to a decision. Why shouldn't she wear it? There would be no one to see. The neighbours on one side were too old to care, and on the other, too newly married and in love to notice. She knew Alan was out, so there would be no need to hide from him.

She put it on. The mirror showed her someone she hardly knew. She met her mother on the landing. 'Is it too brief to wear in the garden, Mum?'

'Of course not, dear. Don't be so shy. Other girls aren't. You look lovely in it. You're really beautiful, Lorrie, when you take the trouble.'

She put her arms round her mother. 'Your flattery's lovely and Mum-like. It makes me feel good to hear it.'

'It's true, Lorrie. It's not just because I'm your mother.'

'Anyway, you look very nice too. Where are you going?'

Mrs. Ferrers was vague in her answer. 'Oh, a run somewhere. I may not be back until after tea. You don't mind getting your own tea, do you?'

Lorraine told her to go and enjoy herself, then she spread out a tartan rug on the lawn and stretched out on it, facing the house, because the sun was in that direction. Lorraine thought she must have slept, because something disturbed her. She opened her eyes, raised her head and looked round. She knew the house was empty and decided it must have been someone next door closing a window.

She put on sunglasses and opened her book. She was so absorbed in it she didn't hear the footsteps until they were almost upon her. She dropped the book, sat up and stared into Alan Darby's face. Sunglasses masked his eyes and the expression in them. Lorraine snatched off her glasses and promptly replaced them. She did not want him to see her eyes, because they would give away her feelings, and at that moment the strength of them terrified her.

She wished he would go away. She wished he would say something, do something, anything to end that stiff hard silence. She groped madly for something to say.

'I—I thought you were out, Mr. Darby.'

'I was, Miss Ferrers. I came back.'

She was imprisoned by her embarrassment, the words she wanted to say were impounded by her lips. Then he spoke and his smile was edged with broken glass. The words seemed to graze her skin.

'Dull, Miss Ferrers? Ordinary? Unexciting? And very, *very* respectable? In *that* outfit?'

She tried to break the barrier imposed by the darkened lenses which hid his eyes. She failed. He walked away, but only a few yards. She saw that he had placed a chair on the lawn, facing the sun. He sat down, opened a book and said,

'I take it you have no objection, Miss Ferrers? Your mother gave me permission to use the garden whenever I liked.'

'I can hardly go against my mother's wishes, Mr. Darby, however much I might want to. You are, after all, her guest, not mine.'

His fingers stiffened the merest fraction, as if he would have liked to force her to swallow her words, then he relaxed them. He had taken off his jacket and removed his tie and his shirt was open to the waist. He sat still for the rest of the afternoon.

Lorraine turned on her front and opened her book again.

34

She tried to concentrate on the words in front of her, but found she could not put him out of her mind. She read and re-read one sentence after another, but it was no use. She could not take a word of it in.

Now and then she stole a look at her companion. She was puzzled. She could not see in him the loud-mouthed, hard-drinking newspaper man she had made herself believe he was. There was something about him, a professional quality, an intellectualism, an air of learning which, she was sure, journalists did not usually possess. A quiet boy, her mother had called him. And there he was, beside her, a quiet man.

Her prejudices, her preconceived ideas, her resentment against him were all crumbling away and taking her peace of mind with them as they fell. She knew then what was happening to her and she was terrified. She had to get her thoughts back under control. She scrambled up, gathered the rug in her arms, picked up her book. He raised his head and watched her, and the more he watched the more confused she became. Her heartbeats had her by the throat and she ran. She ran from the garden, she ran from him, but most of all, she ran away from herself.

A few evenings later, she was making notes for school when the doorbell rang. She thought it was her mother returning from a neighbour's house and wondered why she had not taken the key.

It was Hugh. 'I'm so sorry, Hugh, I must have forgotten——'

He shook his head as he stepped into the hall. 'You didn't forget, Lorraine. I've come to see Alan. He invited me for the evening. Didn't you know?'

'How could I? His private life is nothing to do with me.'

'All right, all right. Don't lose your temper!'

She felt a bit ashamed. 'Sorry, Hugh. Do go up. He must

be expecting you.'

She returned to the dining-room and tried to work. The doorbell rang again. Was it her mother this time?

'Does Mr. Alan Darby live here?'

Lorraine answered the girl on the doorstep. 'He does.'

'Oh good. I thought so. He's expecting me. My name's Margot French. I'm a colleague of his. You must be—Miss Ferrers? He's spoken about you.'

Lorraine nodded and watched as Margot's eyes skated over her, taking in her plain white blouse and shiny brown skirt. 'Yes,' said Miss French, 'I thought you must be.'

Lorraine gathered from the girl's expression just what her colleague had been saying about her. 'Do go up, Miss French. He—he already has a visitor.'

'Yes, I know. He told me he would have someone there he wanted me to meet.'

Lorraine opened her mouth like a fish, and shut it again because no words would come out. Her eyes felt as though they were starting out of their sockets, but by then Alan's visitor was almost up the stairs.

Lorraine shook with anger and she scarcely had control of her pen as she tried to write with it. So it was all pre-arranged, a cosy little chat for three. Her boy-friend, Alan's girl-friend—and Alan! While she, Lorraine, sat downstairs alone, neglected and ignored. She heard the laughter and the talking. She heard the glasses chinking and smelt the cigarette smoke creeping down the stairs.

She remembered how she had looked, the girl called Margot. Not too tall, slim and elegant to her fingertips. She had been wearing a flowing white and black checked cape which almost covered a smart black dress. A small black hat half revealed her auburn hair and her face scarcely needed the skilful make-up she had applied to enhance its beauty.

Beryl Ferrers returned and heard them talking. She decided to make 'the dears' some coffee. 'I'm not taking it up, Mum,' Lorraine told her. 'Hugh's up there.'

'Don't be like that, dear. It's only Alan being friendly. If you were nicer to him ...' She saw the fury on her daughter's face and stopped. She took it up herself and stayed with them for the rest of the evening.

At last she came down, followed by the others. Beryl called out, 'Goodnight, Hugh.'

Lorraine went into the hall, thinking she would do the same. She was just in time to see Hugh disappearing into the darkness with his arm round Margot's shoulders, his face laughing down into hers.

They drove away together in Hugh's car. Lorraine looked up to the landing. Alan was standing there, smiling his slow irritating smile.

'She's attractive, my girl-friend, isn't she, Miss Ferrers? You'd better watch out, or your boy-friend will be losing his heart to her, and then you'll be losing him.'

Lorraine took a deep breath to steady herself. 'If—if his feelings about me are as fickle as that, then—then she can have him!' She ran back into the dining-room and to her horror, she burst into tears.

Later, when the house was quiet, she dragged herself up to bed. As she passed Alan's door she acknowledged in her heart that it was not Hugh she had been crying about.

Alan soon bought himself a car. He told Beryl he had sold his old one before going to live there. When he knew they had a garage, he had decided to buy another car.

It was long, low, cream-coloured and fast, and Ann was the first to sample it. Alan called at her digs to take her to the art exhibition and she told Lorraine afterwards that the car was brand-new.

Lorraine heard her voice in the hall when he brought her back with him. She went out to greet Ann and saw how attractive she looked.

'New dress, Lorraine.' Ann turned like a fashion model. 'Had a super meal,' she whispered. 'Now he's giving me a drink.' She gave a broad wink. 'Coming up?'

'I haven't been invited,' Lorraine answered, her voice flat, and returned to the lounge to watch television.

She watched, but she didn't see a thing. Her thoughts were clattering around her head like beads in a baby's rattle. She could see his plan now. She had refused his offer of a truce and now she was paying the penalty. One by one, methodically, sadistically, he was taking away her friends.

The television swam and distorted in front of her eyes and she switched it off in despair. She said goodnight to her mother and went to bed early. She didn't even hear Ann go home.

Next day at lunch-break, Ann told her all about it. The meal had been wonderful, the art exhibition fun, but most of all she had enjoyed the chat in his room.

'He's so entertaining, Lorraine. You should ask him about his job some time. Have you seen a copy of his paper lately?'

'I never read it. It's a rag.'

'It isn't now. He's done wonders. By the way, he told me there'll be a photo of him in it today. You know, new boy and all that, hot from Fleet Street.'

Lorraine made a silent note to avoid all evening paper sellers on her way home. Ann's next words nearly sent her skating across the room. 'I'm going out with him again, Lorraine.' Ann looked guilty when she saw Lorraine's face. 'Sorry, dear. Would you rather I didn't? Am I letting the side down?'

Somehow Lorraine managed to smile in spite of the jab of almost physical pain which hit her body like a bullet. 'Of course not, Ann. Go and enjoy yourself. Where's it to be this time?'

'He's got four tickets for an audio fair in London. He's invited Hugh, because he's keen on radio, and a girl called Margot's coming, too.'

Lorraine's pain turned into searing anger, but she managed to mask it until Ann had gone. That afternoon she swept into her class and turned in scathing fury on anyone who stepped out of line by making the most insignificant mistake or making the slightest noise. The girls curled up under the lash of her sarcasm and they had never scurried out of the classroom so gladly as they did at the end of her lesson that day.

On her way home she bought a copy of Alan's paper. She took it up to her bedroom, tugged the pages over one by one until she saw his face looking up at her. She seized some scissors, sliced round the photograph and lifted it out. She was on the point of screwing the piece of paper into a tight ball when unaccountably she stopped. In spite of herself she gazed at his face, saw the arched eyebrows, the good mouth, the strong jawline and the keen eyes. As she looked, she saw again the elusive quality which had tormented her that day in the garden. The quiet man was caught by the camera, held still, unsmiling and tantalising in the integrity of character which it revealed, and slowly, surely, her anger died. Gently and with infinite care, she put it into a drawer, deep down where no one would find it.

It was Lorraine's turn to do the cleaning. She did it in rotation with her mother, but somehow she had always managed to get out of cleaning Alan's room, either by 'forgetting' it so that her mother had to do it, or by refusing outright to go in there. That evening her mother went out so she had to face it.

She put on slacks and an old blue sweater and tapped on Alan's door. She willed him to be out. He was in. He opened the door and scowled when he saw the cleaner.

'If it's not convenient——' she said, and turned away.

'Oh, come in and get it over.'

She dragged the cleaner into the room and looked round. 'Oh, it's not too bad. Not as untidy as I thought it might be.'

'What did you expect? Empty whisky bottles all over the place? Ash-trays piled high with cigarette stubs? Women all over the floor?'

'Yes.'

'Sorry to disappoint you. Next time give me notice of arrival and I'll see what I can do.' He shrugged into his jacket. 'I'm going out to my car.'

Lorraine dusted and cleaned and tidied up generally. As she was leaving, Alan returned. 'Finished? Thanks.' He flung himself into a chair. His smile was deliberately provocative. 'Next time, before you come, I'll fill the room with women.'

'That shouldn't be difficult for you.'

'No, it shouldn't. My diary's full of their names and addresses.' He leaned his head back and looked at her through half-lowered lids. 'Women,' he mused, 'shall I tell you what I do with them?' He dragged out his words for greater effect. 'One at a time, I let them into my garden, through the little gate. I let them grow a bit and flower a bit, then, when they're in full bloom, I pluck them out,' he made a pulling movement through the air with his hand, 'and throw them away, like weeds.' He dusted his hands and lifted them to clasp them behind his head. With sardonic eyes he watched her reaction.

One by one her muscles tightened. She said, through stiff lips, 'Oh dear, I shall have to warn Ann, won't I?'

He frowned. 'Ann? You'll do no such thing. Ann and I understand each other pefectly.'

'So,' she thought, 'another door has slammed shut in my face.' She knew she was asking for trouble, but she couldn't stop herself saying, in an uncertain sort of voice, 'What—what would you do about someone like me?'

His face grew into a papier-mâché mask and his eyes closed down. 'You? *You?* I wouldn't even let you into my garden.'

By the time he had finished speaking, she had clamped

down on all her muscles. The only thing that slipped the net was her bottom lip, and that trembled uncontrollably. She turned and went blindly from the room.

The following evening, Hugh called. He seemed to Lorraine to have been avoiding her at school, but when she invited him home that day, he accepted at once.

The evening followed the usual pattern. Lorraine knitted, Hugh skimmed through magazines. They talked now and then of everyday matters. She felt the heaviness between them, the lack of spontaneity, the absence of even a single spark of feeling. Then she remembered his expression as he had looked down at Margot the evening he took her home. She recalled his response to the girl's undoubted charm, saw again his arm round her shoulders, even though he had only just met her. 'He's known me for two years,' she thought miserably, 'and I've forgotten the last time he kissed me on the mouth.'

She knew then that it was over. She put down her knitting and told him so. She spoke haltingly, stumbling over the words. She spoke with humiliation, knowing that in having to say them at all, she was really admitting to herself that, as a woman, she was a dismal failure.

At first, Hugh seemed upset, then relieved. Lorraine made some tea and they drank it. Then they shook hands and Hugh left. She sat for a long time staring at the hearth, seeing nothing, because her eyes were turned inwards in a searching, ruthless attempt at self-examination.

There was a tap on the door. Automatically and without moving her limbs from their lifeless droop, she called, 'Come in.'

Alan opened the door and stood there regarding her. 'Oh, I'm sorry. I thought I heard Hugh's voice.'

'You did. He left ten minutes ago.'

She knew the bleakness was still in her face.

Alan frowned. 'What's the matter? Has something gone

41

wrong between you?'

Lorraine answered dully, 'There was nothing to go wrong. We were friends, nothing more.'

He sat sideways on a chair and contemplated her narrowly. 'Yes, I know what you mean. Every time he came, you sat and knitted, invincible, inviolate, with as much warmth and magnetism about you as a piece of marble, while he sat and read the paper. All purely—and I mean purely—platonic.'

Her sense of failure deepened as she listened to him and she curled her toes to trap the tension which gripped her at the frightening accuracy of his words. She answered sullenly, 'If you must know, yes.'

He said softly, cruelly, his words as toxic as poisoned arrows, 'And you should have seen him responding to Margot.'

She picked up her knitting and flung it down again. 'There's no need to rub salt in the wound,' she choked. 'No need at all.'

He ignored her anger and went on as though she had not spoken. 'And now you're all alone.' The exultation was unmistakable. 'No man in tow, no——'

'Yes, all alone,' she cried out. 'All alone. That was what you wanted, wasn't it? What you were aiming for? Well, now you've succeeded *you* can leave me alone, can't you?'

He could hear the tears in her voice and see the hopelessness of failure in her eyes. Quietly he closed the door behind him.

CHAPTER III

BERYL'S friendship with her employer, James Cornish, seemed to be blooming.

'He'd like to meet you, Lorrie,' she told her daughter one day. 'You don't mind that I'm getting so—friendly with him?'

'Mum,' Lorraine kissed her cheek, 'I'm delighted. Get as friendly with him as you like. Only give me good warning when you want me to move out and find myself a flat, won't you?'

'Don't be silly, Lorrie. I'll always want you here.'

But Lorraine knew there would come a time when she wouldn't. As the days went by, she felt increasingly isolated. 'Everyone has someone,' she thought petulantly, 'except me.' She was glad she had her evening class at the technical college to keep her mind occupied.

One evening in October, her class at the college was changed to a different night for one week. As she took the lift to the third floor, she tried to remember the number of the room which had been set aside for her class.

She collected the class register from the head of department's room and walked along the corridor peering through the glass panels of the doors, hoping to recognise her own students. She came to the end classroom and glanced in quickly. She looked a second time and caught her breath in disbelief. Surely it wasn't Alan Darby lecturing to a class of students! 'It's my stupid imagination,' she chided herself. 'I'm haunted by him wherever I go.'

Then, to make quite sure, she looked again and knew that this time there was no doubt about it. He was there, he was real, and judging by what he had written on the blackboard, he was teaching English. *English!* Only propriety prevented her from thrusting open the door and bursting into the room to denounce him as an impostor in front of the students.

Anger snapped at her heels like a bad-tempered dog all the way back along the corridor. She found her students and apologised for being late. For the remainder of the evening, her mind was split in two. Half of it gave a reasonable, if mechanical lecture on the English language. The other half seethed with indignation that the college authorities had been fooled into taking on to the part-time staff a man who was completely unqualified to do the work he had been engaged for, a newspaperman, a journalist who was incapable of telling the difference between good English and bad.

It did not occur to her that she might meet him when classes closed, so she was quite unprepared for the sight of him in the head of department's room when she returned the class register. He was pulling open a drawer in the desk and pushing his register inside.

Lorraine's instinct was to turn and run, as though she were the one who had no right to be there, but he lifted his head and saw her. Her heartbeats seemed to halt for an agonising moment, then raced crazily as his surprise turned into something else—discomfiture, perhaps, at having been found out?

'Hallo, Miss Ferrers.' His voice was even, controlled. He seemed quite unabashed.

'Good evening, Mr. Darby,' she replied levelly.

She walked over to the desk and he moved back slightly to allow her to push her register into the drawer on top of his. Then they looked at each other as if uncertain what the next move should be.

Alan broke the silence. 'Would you like a lift home?'

No explanation, no apology, just a casual offer of a ride in his car. His self-possession and his impenitent attitude almost goaded her into an angry refusal, but she changed

44

her mind.

'Thank you, yes,' she answered, making her tone as condescending as possible. He raised an eyebrow and a flick of amusement touched his mouth as they left the room together.

They walked in silence down three flights of stairs and out into the college car park. They drove home without exchanging a word and when Alan drew up in the driveway, they both got out of the car together.

Lorraine took out her key and opened the front door. Alan followed her into the hall. Then he spoke.

'Well, Miss Ferrers, your silence has been eloquent. Out with it. It's obvious something's eating you. What crime have I committed now?'

'Crime? You're so right, Mr. Darby.' Her eyes, ignited by the strength of her feelings, blazed into his and she became conscious at the same time of a feeling of relief that she could at last talk her anger out. 'What I should like to know is this. Are the college authorities aware that they have on their part-time staff an impostor, a teacher who is completely unqualified to do the job for which, in good faith, they are paying him? Someone, in fact, whose sole qualification for the subject he is teaching is that he earns his living by dabbling in journalistic trivialities and petty gossip——'

He took her up, brows lifted, contempt and amusement fighting for possession of his eyes, 'And whose prime occupation in life is to pander to the uneducated majority of the population, and in so doing reduce the English language to the level of inanities and words of one syllable? In other words, me?'

'Of course. Who else?' She tried not to be frightened by the crouching anger which sprang, tiger-swift, into his eyes.

'So what do you intend to do about it? Turn informer? Denounce me?'

She attempted to meet his challenge, but her eyes

45

wavered and fell beneath the derision in his. Then his eye-lids drooped and his voice became liltingly soft. 'You really are a first-class little bitch. There's no other word to describe you.'

She raised her head and saw the relish in his smile. 'All right, Miss Ferrers, go ahead, do your worst, then report back to me. I'll be interested to know what the college authorities have to say when they hear your denunciation of me.'

He strode up the stairs, stopped half-way and came down again. 'No, I've changed my mind. I'll save you the trouble.'

'You mean—you'll tell them yourself? You'll resign?'

'No, I will not resign. I'll tell *you* something instead. Stand here, Miss Ferrers.' He grasped her arm and moved her forcibly under the hall light. 'Here, where I can see your face.'

She was puzzled by his gloating expression, the anticipation of pleasure on his face. She was not puzzled for long.

'I, my dear Miss Ferrers, am better qualified than you are.'

As Lorraine opened her mouth to protest, he held up his hand. 'Be quiet, please, I haven't finished.' Her frown deepened as he continued, speaking each word with loving deliberation, 'For your information, I hold a University degree. If I chose to do so, I would be entitled to put after my name, every time I wrote it, M.A. (Oxon.) In other words, I read English at Oxford University, graduated with first-class honours and stayed on to qualify for my higher degree.' He smiled with diabolical satisfaction. 'Yes, I thought that would bring the colour to your cheeks. That's why I wanted to watch your reaction. I wanted to watch you squirm with embarrassment, as you're now doing.' He advanced towards her, hands thrust into his jacket pockets. She tried to stammer out an apology, but he did not give her the chance.

He stood, rigid and menacing, directly in front of her. 'I ought to force you to retract every single charge you've made against me, every miserable calculated insult and accusation you've thrown at my head ever since I set foot in this house. In fact, I ought to make you grovel,' he growled out the word, 'at my feet and plead for forgiveness.'

She opened her mouth for the second time to apologise, but all that came out was, 'But—but why——?'

'Why keep it quiet? Why not tell the world? Because in my profession—yes, I'm talking about journalism—in my *profession*,' he ground out the word for greater impact, 'it wouldn't do at all to flaunt my academic achievements in front of my colleagues. They'd either look upon me as an insufferable bighead, or hound me out of my job as an inexperienced, unqualified academic, posing as a journalist and,' he narrowed his eyes dangerously as he quoted her own words back at her, 'quite incapable of doing the job for which, in good faith, they are paying me.' He smiled nastily. 'Ironic, isn't it? Paradoxical, almost, considered in the light of all you've said about me. So I play it down, that University background of mine.'

Conscious now that she was at a complete disadvantage and that he had undoubtedly gained the upper hand in their relationship, she stammered, 'But why—why, with such a good degree, did you——'

He cut in, 'Why did I become a journalist? Why didn't I pursue a more learned occupation? I'll tell you.' He took out a cigarette, and with irritating slowness, kindled the flame of his lighter and drew on the cigarette before he spoke again. She watched his every movement, still unable to believe all he had told her. He leaned sideways against the end of the banister rail, and contemplated her, his expression revealing that he was still enjoying her look of bewildered defeat.

'Straight from University, I went into teaching. M'm, I

thought that would surprise you. But after a couple of years of daily grind and keeping naughty little boys in order, I couldn't stand it any longer. I couldn't stand the stifling, restricting atmosphere of an obsolescent school whose very building was an anachronism. I couldn't tolerate the narrow outlook of my colleagues—people like you, Miss Ferrers, who didn't hesitate to moralise at length on subjects quite beyond their knowledge and comprehension. People who, like you, refused to let the fresh air of new ideas into their subjects and teaching methods.'

He lounged against the banisters and watched her narrowly as she groped for the support of the wall behind her.

'One day, Miss Ferrers,' he blew a cloud of smoke towards the ceiling, 'I'll give you a lesson—in how to teach English, the English of the latter half of the twentieth century. In fact,' he smiled and his mind stroked a pleasing thought like a hand caressing a kitten, 'in fact, you could come to the college next week and sit in on the lecture I give to my evening students. You might pick up some valuable hints to help you, not only to improve your own knowledge of English, but also to enhance your own teaching performance.'

He swung round and was up the stairs in a few strides, leaving Lorraine limp and stupefied, leaning sideways against the wall.

Lorraine said to Ann in the staff room, as they were eating their sandwiches during lunch-break, 'How's your heart?'

She started. 'My heart?' She searched madly round her ribs, pressed her fingers left of centre and sighed with relief. 'It's still there, hammering loud and clear. You had me worried, love.'

Lorraine said, long-sufferingly, ignoring her little joke, 'Perhaps I should have asked, how's your affair going?'

'Now you've got me excited, and that's bad for my heart.

48

Tell me, what affair, and who with?'

'Alan Darby, of course.'

Ann hooted with laughter. 'You can't be serious. There's nothing in it, love. Discount all rumours.'

'But he told me you understood each other.'

She frowned, considered Lorraine's words, then said, 'M'm, I'm not sure, but I think I know what he means.'

'So you're just good friends?'

'No, not even that, dear.'

'Then why does he keep asking you to go out with him?'

Ann stuffed half a sandwich into her mouth and talked through it, fluffing out crumbs all over her skirt. 'To be honest, I suspect I'm—er—a sprat to catch a mackerel, as they say.' She brushed the crumbs away thoughtfully.

'I supppose you mean you're the bait to lure Margot French into Alan's net?'

Ann swallowed hugely and reached for her vacuum flask. 'Could be, could be.'

Lorraine persisted, 'So he's using you to make Margot jealous?'

She couldn't keep the dullness from her tone and Ann looked at her shrewdly, but all she said was, 'Could be' three times over.

'Incidentally, Lorraine,' Ann went on, 'you know I'm going to the audio fair in London tomorrow? It'll be an intriguing situation. I don't know whether I'm supposed to tag along with Hugh or partner our tame Lord Beaverbrook. I'll have fun watching the two men scrapping over the fair Margot. I, no doubt, will be landed with the boy who didn't get the girl.'

'Do you mind?'

'Mind? My dear girl, I'll relish it. I'm fire-proof at my age. I never was the marrying kind, you know that. I love the odd pin-up boy, and adore handsome men in the flesh, but my adoration would never stand the test of marriage. So don't worry about me. All the same, I've bought myself a new outfit. I'm damned if I'll let Madam Margot make me feel like a left-over from a jumble sale.' She eyed Lorraine. 'Incidentally, go thou and do likewise, love. Treat yourself to some new clothes. Take advice from Auntie. Don't let yourself turn into a frump, Lorraine. You might regret it all your life. It takes a woman like Margot to make us also-rans conscious of our dowdiness. I mean it.' Her face was serious.

'If you say so, Auntie, I might do just that.'

'Good.' She stood up and crumpled her sandwich paper, aimed for the waste-paper basket and hit the target. 'The sooner the better. I'll make sure you keep your word.'

That evening James Cornish, Beryl's employer, called at the house. Lorraine met him in the kitchen. She judged that he was in his early fifties, perhaps a year or two older than her mother. He was slim and his greying hair sprang spike-like from his scalp. His face was creased with laughter lines and he seemed to possess a personality which encompassed and cherished whoever came into contact with him. Lorraine was not surprised that her mother had grown fond of him. He took Lorraine's hand and refused to let it go until she had kissed him on both cheeks. Then he kissed her in the same way. He held her away from him, praised her lavishly and with blatant flattery and put his arm round Beryl's shoulders.

'A daughter to be proud of,' he said, and they exchanged warm smiles.

As they left the house, their pleasure in each other was there for all to see, and Lorraine had to quell a rush of self-pity so strong it made her sway like a tree in a gale.

Ann was the first to arrive at the house next morning. It was Saturday and she was going with the others to the audio fair. She went into the dining-room and showed Lorraine her new pale blue suit.

'New shoes too?' Lorraine asked.

'Yes, dear. And gloves and handbag. And I won't rest until you get yourself something decent to wear, too. Just look at you, all frump from chin to the end of your big toe! And why *do* you pull your hair back like that, Lorraine? Wear it loose, do yourself a favour.'

Lorraine drew in her lips. 'Not on your life, Ann. Not even for you. My hair stays as it is. Who is there for me to make myself nice for?'

'You'd be surprised,' Ann muttered cryptically, going into the hall.

She went upstairs and soon after that Margot arrived, followed closely by Hugh. Lorraine heard them upstairs laughing over their drinks and it was half an hour before they came down. She stood in the hall and watched them, unaware of the wistfulness in her eyes.

First came Margot, impeccably dressed, tiny white hat topping a trim green and white outfit. She turned at the foot of the stairs and put out her hand to Hugh who was following her. Then came Ann and, last, Alan.

He had something in his hand and he crossed the hall to stand in front of Lorraine. She looked at him questioningly and lowered her eyes. He was holding out a book which appeared to be on the teaching of modern English.

'Occupy yourself reading that, Miss Ferrers. Incidentally, it's returnable.'

She took it from him as though he were handing her the Koh-i-noor diamond. She thanked him and hoped that he could see the gratitude which she tried to put into her eyes. She thought he must have done because when he turned away, his smile was—almost—kindly.

As they proceeded down the path to the gate, Margot was holding one of Hugh's hands and one of Alan's. Her sophisticated naïveté left Lorraine breathless with admiration. 'How does she do it?' she wondered, battling with a feeling of inadequacy which, though usually dormant, had been prodded into wakefulness by Margot's overwhelming self-confidence. She felt intensely then her own lack of charm, her too-serious disposition which could never hope to attract the interest or the love of any man.

She took a crumb of comfort from the wry look which Ann threw over her shoulder. She saw the broad wink and the eyes turned upwards, but in spite of that mock despair, Lorraine knew that Ann was enjoying herself. She closed the front door thankful to be the odd one out at home rather than tagging along behind the others like Ann.

That afternoon Lorraine went to the town, drew a large sum of money from her savings account and ransacked the department stores for new clothes.

The following day was Sunday and Lorraine felt the urge to get away on her own. After lunch she called from the front door, 'I'm off to the park, Mum.'

Beryl came from the kitchen. 'You look nice, dear. I like those pink trousers. And your jacket. It's chunky-knit, isn't it? They're a good match, Lorrie. Where did you get them?'

Lorraine told her the name of the department store.

'How much?' her mother asked and when Lorraine told her, she whistled. 'My, when you make up your mind to do something, you do it big, don't you? But I'm glad. It's more than time you had some new things.'

'It was Ann really,' Lorraine laughed. 'She made me ashamed of my old things. There's not much left in my savings account, though.'

'Never mind, you'll soon build that up again.'

A door closed upstairs and Lorraine realised Alan must have heard all they had been saying, but for once she didn't care.

''Bye, Mum. Have a good time with James.' She went out and closed the door behind her.

Lorraine was glad to find that the park was almost empty. She climbed the hill and walked along the ridge, breathing deeply and filling her lungs. This was good, she felt, this was freedom. This was fresh air she wanted to toss down her throat like vintage wine and imbibe to the point of intoxication. Her eyes drank in the rise and fall of the distant hills, drew back nearer home to recoil a little at the creeping menace of urbanisation.

As she stared around, hands clasped behind her, an aircraft flying overhead droned its long-drawn-out and unmistakable message. 'You are a-lone,' it seemed to say, 'a-lo-one for the rest of your life.' She walked, hands pushed down hard into her pockets, kicking idly at odd tufts of grass. She knew she had to face it, she had to grow reconciled to the fact. Others had—look at Ann. She seemed to prefer her solitary state now. 'The difference is,' Lorraine told herself, and the thought struck her like a sudden blow, 'I love a man.' But other lonely people might have loved at some time, too, hopelessly of course, like her. If they had recovered and become resigned to losing, never winning, against more attractive women, then so could she.

It was the end of October. She lay down under a tree, leafless now, stark and stiffly branching to the sky. Despite the afternoon sun, weak and dull gold, the air was chilly. She rolled on to her front and bent her legs behind her, kicking them up and down like a child. She took a few dead leaves in her hand and crushed them, letting them fall in bits to the ground, brushing off the last clinging pieces from her palm. Then she raised her arms, folded them to form a pillow and rested her cheek on them. She lay there for a long time in perfect peace.

Footsteps were climbing the hill. The tread was firm and deliberate. Those feet knew exactly where they were going. She willed them to go past and leave her alone again. She wanted no company but her own. She could have cried out when they stopped beside her.

'Miss Ferrers?'

It could not be, it mustn't be ... Her head jerked round

like a puppet's and she took in the heavy shoes, casual trousers and rough jacket, the high-necked sweater and the face above them all, serious, unsmiling, looking down at her.

'Nice day,' the lips said. She nodded. 'Warm for the time of year,' the lips persisted.

She shivered and nodded. Anything to make him go, anything to stop him shattering her hard-won peace of mind, anything to make him, of all people, stop tormenting her and leave her alone.

He threw himself down beside her and rested on his elbow. She rolled away from him and tore at unoffending blades of grass with restless, sadistic fingers. Her tongue was roped up, tied tight, never to move again. She felt her inadequacy more than ever then, her inability to communicate with any member of the opposite sex, especially this one. She had nothing inside her to charm a man with her talk, to move him to laughter at her empty chatter, no way of looking at him to make him want to touch and love her.

As she lay there with Alan beside her, she experienced again that desolate feeling that, as a woman, she was a miserable failure. She had nothing to give any man. He must surely see that now, she thought, so why didn't he go? She heard a movement beside her and stiffened, but he had only moved to lie full length. They were still for a long time.

'Why are you treating me as though I were invisible?'

She rolled round to face him, eyes open wide. 'What do you mean?'

'Aren't we on speaking terms?'

She shook her head. 'I just couldn't think of anything to say.'

'Oh, I see. Well, let me rack my brains for inspiration. I'm not usually lost for words.' He scratched his head elaborately. 'Ah, I know. Did you have a look at the book I

54

lent you yesterday?'

'Yes, thank you, I read it.'

He raised his head. 'You mean you finished it, from cover to cover?'

'Well,' she felt defensive, 'I had nothing else to do.'

'You were on your own all day?'

'Except for going shopping, yes.'

He was silent. She couldn't tell him that she had pretty well re-stocked her entire wardrobe, using the savings she had accumulated so painstakingly over the years.

'What did you think of the book?'

'I liked it very much.'

'Good. We must talk about it some time.'

Lorraine knew he didn't mean it. She knew his promise was a thing of the moment, that he had no intention of keeping it. There could never be any interchange of ideas between them, because he had shut her out. 'You?' he'd said. 'You? I wouldn't even let you in.' His 'garden' was so much out of reach, it might as well have been in Eden.

They lapsed into silence again. She lay back beside him.

'Your turn.'

She turned her head in inquiry.

'To talk.'

'Oh, I see.' She laughed. 'Well—er—how did you enjoy the audio fair?'

'Fine, thanks. Ann walked so far she said she wanted to take her feet off.'

Lorraine laughed again. 'Yes, that sounds like Ann.' She paused, then asked, 'Margot?'

'Oh, she would enjoy anything. She has that tremendous capacity for giving, and in life you usually only get back what you give, in the long run.' That was so true, it silenced Lorraine. 'I have nothing to give,' she told herself, 'so I get nothing back.'

'Half-way through,' he went on, 'we swopped partners.'

She laughed.

'What's so funny?'

'Next best thing to swopping wives.'

'Ah yes.' He rolled over towards her, and she felt that his face was far too near. 'Does that idea appeal?'

'Wife-swopping?' She shook her head emphatically. 'Definitely no.'

'So if you ever married, you'd stick to your man for life?'

'If he was a good man, yes. But the problem will never arise with me. I'm a hundred per cent certain I'll never marry. I'm not composed of the necessary ingredients.'

He stood up. 'It's time we went.' He took her hand and hauled her up. She would have moved away, but he stopped her. His hands rested lightly on her shoulders and she wondered what he was going to do. He looked at her face, devoid of make-up, then he moved his hand to the back of her neck. With a quick flick of the wrist he had untied the ribbon which was pulling her hair tightly back from her face. Her hair fell down to her shoulders and over her cheeks. She put up an agitated hand to push it back, but he stopped her.

'No, no, don't touch. Leave it like that. Permanently.' He pushed the ribbon into his pocket.

'Please let me have that back.'

'Not on your life. No girl should be as unkind to herself as you are.'

They walked down the hill. There was nothing more to say.

'You aren't exactly a chatterbox, are you?'

She took offence and showed it. 'If you don't like my company, you can do the other thing. I didn't invite you to tag along.'

'Prickly as a hedgehog, too.'

'I'm sorry I can't produce the scintillating conversation you desire to amuse you and keep you charmed and interested like Margot does.'

He said nothing, but Lorraine was sure he was smiling, which goaded her still more. 'You forget I'm just a dull, respectable old schoolmarm . . .'

A hand was clamped over her mouth, and she nearly bit into it in her fury. Instead, she prised it off and ran away.

As soon as she arrived home, she searched in a drawer for another ribbon. She found a red one and pulled her hair back tighter than ever, trying it securely into position. She sat on her bed, trying to gather her scattered wits. She felt disturbed and restless. What was happening to her? Where was that peace of mind she had discovered while she was on the hill?

As she went on to the landing, Alan reached the top of the stairs. He looked at her hair and narrowed his eyes. She had to pass him to get to the stairs and he allowed her to do so. There was a movement at the back of her neck and her hands shot round in a protective gesture. The ribbon had gone again. Furious now, she turned, her hair swinging round her cheeks.

'Give me back my ribbon!'

He held it high and out of reach. 'It's mine,' he taunted, 'my prize.'

The blood in her veins was scalding her. 'I shall only find another.'

'I'll take that, too.'

'I'll—I'll pin it back into a bun, with hairpins.'

'Then I shall just have the pleasure of removing them one by one.'

She blazed, 'You think I'd just stand there and let you?'

'You wouldn't be able to stop me. I—er—have my methods.' He went on softly, 'And who said anything about standing?'

His malevolent grin roused her to a fury she had never felt before, a fury which took possession of her and was beyond her control. She moved up to him, raised her clenched fists and started to pound his chest. He gripped them and held them away from him and laughed in her face. She wanted to use her teeth, her feet, claw at him with her fingernails, anything to get even with him. She tried to free herself, but the more she struggled the tighter his hold became. Tears of frustration blinded her.

Then she came to her senses. She drooped. He let her go. She mumbled an apology and walked down the stairs. She knew that she had almost crossed the threshold into uncharted seas and she was terror-stricken at the strength of the emotions he had aroused in her. He went into his room, her ribbon still in his hand.

CHAPTER IV

LORRAINE was marking essays in the dining-room one evening when Alan walked in uninvited. 'Busy?' he asked.

'That's obvious,' she snapped.

'I'm very welcome, aren't I?'

He stood beside her and she grew taut. He bent over her shoulder and started reading the essay she was marking. She had given it almost full marks. As he read, she felt a hand moving over her hair which was hanging loose round her neck, because she had given up the fight.

She shook the hand away violently and he looked down at her and laughed. He knew exactly what he was doing. She sensed a change of tactics on his part. She guessed that the phase of isolating her from all her friends had passed. 'Now,' she thought bitterly, 'he's tormenting me at every opportunity.' To have him close was a torture in itself. It was a feeling so new and so worrying that she did not know how to handle it. Every time he approached she became irritable and there seemed to be nothing she could to about it.

'That essay—you've given it a high mark.'

'Yes, because I think it deserves it.'

'Who wrote it?'

'A girl in my class.' She named her.

'Know what I'd do with it? I'd get a pencil—thus,' he took hers from her fingers and ran it through half a dozen words, 'and thus,' before she could stop him, he had done the same to two or three sentences, 'and I'd hand it back and tell her to rewrite it.' He flung the pencil down. 'I'd sub out the lot. It's atrocious.'

Her hand was shaking with indignation. 'Now look at the mess you've made.' She took up a rubber and tried in vain to erase the thick black pencil marks. 'I wish you'd mind your own business.'

Instead of taking offence, he drew up a chair. 'Where's another one?'

She put her arms protectively round the other exercise books. 'You've no right to touch these. It's my job to mark them, not yours.'

'All right, I promise not to put pencil to paper, although the temptation to do so will be overwhelming. Now will you please let me look at them? It's years since I read adolescent outpourings like this. It'll be good for my soul to refresh my memory.' He held out his hand pleadingly. 'Please? I've promised.'

With considerable reluctance, she passed the pile of books to him. He drew his chair nearer the table and closer to Lorraine's. She moved away slightly, but he merely closed the gap. She knew he was doing it for the purpose, so she gritted her teeth and made herself stay put, with his arm pressing against hers. When she couldn't stand his nearness any longer, she started to inch away again. But he hooked his foot round the leg of her chair and she was imprisoned on that spot.

'Keep still,' he ordered. 'I can't concentrate with you fidgeting like that.' He read on. 'Ah, now this effort is good.' He turned the page and saw the low mark she had allotted to it. '*What?* You're out of your mind, woman. This is good stuff.'

'Good? It's terrible. The grammar's shocking, the slang must have originated in the gutter, she breaks all the rules...'

'But look at it. The language is good up-to-date pungent stuff. It's written in the modern idiom and it's language everyone is using all around you, only you're too deaf—wilfully deaf—to hear it.'

'But everyday speech is not the language of English essays. The construction is far too loose, too slovenly——'

'I tell you, this is good. It's not stilted and stripped bare of originality. This girl's obviously resisted with all her strength the deadly hand of the orthodox teaching methods you must have been dosing them with like out of date medicine. I'd give this girl a job as a junior reporter any time she liked to apply.'

He began to read another. 'That statement is incorrect for a start. Don't you teach them to get their facts right? It's one of the first rules of reporting.'

'But teachers of English don't deal in facts. We deal with imagination, well-expressed opinions——'

'Opinions? But you have to give them the facts before they can begin to form their own opinions.'

She shook her head, now quite out of her depth. 'If I brighten up their work too much, if I give them ideas which are too challenging and essay subjects that are too thought-provoking and topical, their parents would want to know why. They would call it a decline in the school's educational standards, and twist things round somehow so as to cast doubts on the teacher's morals.'

'Then you'll just have to educate the parents, won't you?' He read a few more essays then pushed the pile aside. 'Your treatment of these literary efforts tells me all I want to know about your prowess as a teacher of English. It's nil. You've obviously read the rule book from cover to cover and you haven't got the guts to budge from those rules one iota.' He turned and looked at her flushed face as though she were an interesting exhibit in a museum. 'You're one of those creatures I left teaching to get away from, because I couldn't stand their bigoted unreasoning minds.'

She banged her fist on the table, unable to endure his provocation any longer. 'Will you go out and leave me alone?' Her self-confidence was ebbing fast, her well-established ideas on the teaching of English were losing their identity and being churned up and thrown about like ingredients in an electric mixer.

'When I've finished.' He smiled at the hostility in her eyes and saw something across the table. He stretched out his hand and picked it up before she could stop him. 'What's this? An article?' He saw the writer's name and grinned diabolically. 'Ah, a piece by the English teacher herself. Now,' he rubbed his hands, 'this should be interesting.'

'That's my contribution as editor of the school magazine.' She tried to snatch it from him, but he caught her hands and held them prisoner.

Then he threw back his head and laughed. '*You*—the editor? That's the story of the year.'

She tried to tug her hands away. 'I haven't given you permission to read it.'

'Haven't you? Never mind, I didn't ask.'

He started to read it and she slumped beside him. He released her hands immediately. She held her breath while he read it to the end. He put it down and she looked at him expectantly. 'Well?'

He turned sideways and hooked his elbow over the back of his chair. 'Well. What can I say?'

'Is it—is it terrible?'

He laughed at her anxiety, her child-like plea for reassurance.

'Yes,' he said, reaching for her pencil, 'it's terrible. But that's only what I would have expected. But,' he offered her a crumb of comfort, 'some of the ideas are good.' The pencil hovered over the first sentence. He looked at her, eyebrows raised. 'May I?'

She nodded, holding herself in and wincing in advance at what that pencil would do to her precious editorial.

'Yes, you need to be worried,' he said, without looking at her. 'When I've finished with this, you won't recognise it.'

She watched him work. She watched his professionalism, saw the pencil delete, write in, alter the order of words, shorten sentences. She watched the operation like a patient undergoing surgery under a local anaesthetic. She felt numbed and as she watched the crossings-out, the cuts and the rude remarks he wrote in the margin, she knew he must be hurting her, but she didn't feel a thing—until he pushed the finished article across to her and the anaesthetic wore off.

It was almost unrecognisable, but she knew that it had been improved beyond measure. She turned her eyes full on him and met his gaze, which was drawing back from hers with mock-anxiety. 'Am I forgiven?' He got up and went to the door. 'On second thoughts, I'd better get out of here before I have to ward off another onslaught on my person. I'm considering suing you for assault and battery as it is.'

He grinned provocatively and went out.

Lorraine was getting ready to go to Ann's digs, to help her with the hem of a dress she was making. She was wearing a new tartan skirt and a white roll-necked sweater.

Her mother appeared at the bedroom door. 'You do look nice, Lorrie. I told you you were a nice shape. That jumper shows it off.' She turned on her cajoling tone. 'Borrow some of my make-up, dear. Go on, make the best of yourself while you're young.'

She didn't wait for an answer. She collected her foundation, eye-shadow and mascara and took it to her daughter's room. Lorraine used some of it—the eye-shadow and a new shade of lipstick. She let her mother pencil in her eyebrows. Alan opened his door and Beryl called to him,

'Come in and see my beautiful daughter now, Alan.'

'No, don't, Mum,' Lorraine hissed, but it was too late. He sauntered into the bedroom and stood with a half smile watching her run a comb through her hair.

'Turn round, Lorrie, and let him see you properly.' She gave Lorraine a gentle push and she turned.

His expression brought back to her the day he had stood on the doorstep for the first time. He looked her over thoroughly, took her to pieces and put her together again in the space of a few seconds. Those take-apart eyes were hooded and unreadable. Lorraine flushed and turned back to the mirror. She watched his reflection and he nodded slowly. 'A metamorphosis,' he murmured.

Beryl looked at him uncertainly. 'You mean she's changed a lot?'

'Beyond recognition.' He inspected at one glance the contents of the room, including the bed. 'Going out?' he asked casually.

'She's going to Ann's,' her mother answered for her.

He looked interested. 'Give her my love, will you?' He wandered out.

Ann welcomed her with a sweeping bow and praised her appearance lavishly. 'My word, Lorraine, you're a different person. I hate to say "I told you so", but I'm saying it all the same. You're even a match for our Margot nowadays. I mean it, Lorraine, so stop shaking your head. Any reaction from—er—certain quarters?'

Lorraine knew whom she meant and flushed.

'Come on, tell Auntie. What did he say?'

'He called it a—metamorphosis.'

'He did?' Ann's face glowed. 'There you are. I'll have to say it again—I told you so.'

'Coming from him, it doesn't mean a thing, Ann. I doubt if he's got a streak of sincerity in him.' As she made the statement she felt a twinge of conscience, because she knew it was not true, but for some reason she desperately wanted to convince herself it was. 'Anyway, let's get on with your dress. That's far more important.'

Ann stood on the table and turned slowly while Lorraine pinned up the hem to the required length. They had a cup of tea and Lorraine went home, leaving Ann to get on with her sewing.

She let herself into the house and heard music coming from Alan's room. She stood on the landing and listened. It was the New World Symphony by Dvorak and it was one of her favourites. She stayed there a long time. It was during one of the quiet passages that a floorboard creaked under her feet. She held her breath, hoping Alan had not heard but his door was flung open. He looked annoyed. 'What are you doing there?'

'I'm sorry, I was only listening to the music.' She walked away, but he was after her and pulling her into his room before she knew what was happening. He closed the door, pushed her into an armchair and said, through tight teeth, 'Now shut up and let me listen.'

Alan closed his eyes and Lorraine watched him. His face in repose was serious and wholly good. He was there again, that quiet man, the man who disturbed and aroused her more than any man she had ever met. He opened his eyes and looked straight at her as if he were trying to read her thoughts.

She turned her head away, resting her cheek against a cushion. She wanted to close the gap between them and throw herself upon him and tell him he must never let her go. She gripped the arms of the chair and moved restlessly. The music was coming to an end and she tried to lose herself and her wayward thoughts in it.

He turned off the radio and she started to rise. 'No, don't go,' he said. 'I want to play you a record.' He pulled out his record player. 'It's a very different piece of music from the last. It's called "My love's like a red, red rose". You probably know it.' She nodded and he went on, 'Robert Burns wrote the words and I want you to take particular note of them.' He smiled oddly. 'Their message should hold a special appeal for you.' He lowered the disc on to the turntable and set it going.

The song was sweet and haunting and Lorraine listened intently to the words.

> 'As fair art thou, my bonnie lass,
> So deep in love am I——'

65

The strong clear voice of the singer filled the room and Lorraine closed her eyes, gripped by a longing she could hardly bear.

> '*And I will love thee still, my dear,*
>   *Till a' the seas gang dry.*'

She looked across at Alan and found that he was searching her face with a curiously intent expression. As she met his eyes, the strength of her emotions shocked her. Swiftly she fought to regain control. The song went on,

> '*Till a' the seas gang dry, my dear,*
>   *And the rocks melt wi' the sun;*
> *I will love thee still, my dear,*
>   *While the sands of life shall run.*'

The music ended, the playing arm lifted. The room was still. Lorraine looked at Alan and found that he was looking at her. Their gaze held and her heart turned over.

He broke the spell with the cynicism which stained his next words. 'An example of your sort of morality. Devotion for life to the man you marry.' He leaned forward. 'Let me hear you say it again.'

Obediently and without understanding why, she repeated the words he had put into her mouth that day on the hill.

'If I ever married, I would stick to my man for life—provided he was a good man.'

Alan nodded and sank back, satisfied.

'Why did you want me to repeat it?'

'Why? Partly because it's so rare to hear it from a young woman in this decadent age, and partly'—he paused—'so that, in the years to come—if I'm still acquainted with you—I can remind you of it and keep you to it, when you're married to the man of your choice.'

'And you're still tending the flowers in your garden. And

plucking them out when they're in full bloom.'

'As you say,' his eyes narrowed, 'plucking them out in full bloom.'

She lowered her voice. 'I'm glad I'll never be a flower in your garden.'

His voice was equally quiet. 'No, you'll never be that. Obviously our moralities don't dovetail at all.' He smiled. 'But what else can you expect? I'm a journalist, after all, and as everyone knows, journalists are immoral devils.' He grinned broadly.

She pulled herself quickly out of the chair, but he came over and pushed her down. 'Have a drink.'

'Well, I——'

'Sherry?' He opened a bottle, poured from it and put a glass into her hand. 'Don't look so scared. I haven't got designs on you—at the moment.' His eyes were lazy. 'The idea appeals, though.' He drank. 'Just imagine the head-lines—banner headlines—"Lodger Journalist seduces drunken Girl Teacher". My word, what a story!' He became serious. 'Tell me about your school.'

She told him, with only half of her mind paying attention to what she was saying. The other half was wide-eyed with astonishment that she was sitting there in his room, chatting to him as her friends had done. And what was more astonishing, he actually seemed to want her company. No doubt he had been forced to choose between a thoroughly boring, lonely evening—and his landlady's daughter. Obviously the latter had been the lesser of two evils.

'The school is ancient and traditional in outlook,' she told him, 'housed in an equally ancient building. Doctrinaire, orthodox headmistress and almost as old as the place itself.' He laughed. 'Girls beautifully drilled——'

'Mentally as well as physically?'

'That's right. Head girl who has toed the line all the way up the school——'

'Not an original idea in her head?'

She nodded. 'School discipline rigid and unchanged for half a century——'

'And likely to remain so for the next half century?'

'Yes again. Teachers with narrow outlooks——'

'No vision?'

'Yes, they all seem to come from the same mould, all petty-minded and——'

He broke in, 'M'm. Just as you used to be.'

She began to get the drift of what had been happening. Those ideas she had just expressed so lucidly, were they really hers? She realised then, with some annoyance, how cleverly he had been egging her on, putting words into her mouth . . . 'As *I* used to be?'

'Yes, before I got to work on you. I've woken you up, made you aware that time inevitably moves on and changes things. Be honest, I'm right, aren't I?'

She didn't care if he was. She stood up, determined to go this time. She thought she saw a flick of disappointment in his eyes, but she realised she had been mistaken because when she turned at the door and said, 'Goodnight, Mr. Darby, and thanks for the drink,' he bowed deeply from the waist.

'Goodnight, Miss Ferrers.' She saw his sardonic grin and knew he was mocking her. 'Your company has been appreciated. No doubt you're thoroughly relieved at having escaped from my clutches all in one piece. Next time, you may not be so lucky. After all, you never can tell with journalists, can you?'

She walked across the landing, closed her bedroom door behind her and shut him out.

At school Ann asked, 'Has Alan mentioned the centenary celebrations to you?' Lorraine looked blank, so Ann went on, 'His newspaper's holding a press ball to celebrate its hundred years of existence.' She named a large hotel in the town where it was to be held. 'He's invited me to go with him.'

68

Lorraine stuffed her jealousy deep into a pocket of her mind and asked, casually, 'Are you going?'

'Me, dearie? No thanks. Not my cup of tea at all. I told him to invite you instead.'

'What did he say?'

'Oh,' she waved her arm vaguely, 'he didn't think he would. He mumbled something about the way you're always quarrelling with him and didn't want his evening spoilt.' Lorraine found that she was almost mutilating her bottom lip in an effort to keep it still.

'He said,' Ann was saying, 'that he would offer a couple of tickets to your mother instead. He told me Hugh was taking Margot, so he would have to find another partner himself.'

Lorraine turned pale under the desolation which swept over her and Ann, looking at her, commented sadly, 'It's like that, is it, love?'

Lorraine took a hold on her emotions. 'Like what?'

Ann shook her head. 'I don't think you'll get anywhere, Lorraine. I doubt if he's the "settle down and marry the girl" type.'

Lorraine stopped pretending and sighed. 'I know that, Ann. I'm reconciled.'

'It's a pity, though,' Ann said thoughtfully, 'I honestly thought that if you started to make more of yourself and dressed up a bit, things might have been different between you.'

'Well, I did, and it hasn't worked, has it?'

Ann shrugged. 'You never can tell with men. Funny creatures. You know, when I visited Alan in his room, we seemed to spend half the time talking about you. Somehow he always managed to bring a reference to you into the conversation. I began to think——'

'I can tell you why,' Lorraine cut in bitterly. 'I get on his nerves so much that the only way he can get me out of his system is to talk about me disparagingly behind my back.'

Ann frowned. 'It wasn't quite like that, dear——' She looked at her watch. 'Time we were off.' They parted to go to their classes.

Lorraine was trying to brighten up her teaching sessions. Somehow at the back of her mind, she was conscious of the idea that it might please Alan. It would be something to tell him, she told herself, something to make him notice her and stop dismissing her as the nonentity he obviously thought she was. She had started to take his advice, and introduce more variety and imagination into the work she gave the girls to do. They seemed to be responding by showing more interest and by thinking of new ideas without being prompted too often by her.

A few evenings later, Beryl offered Lorraine one of her tickets to the press ball. 'I don't want it, dear,' she said. 'I'm past that sort of thing. I asked James, but he said he didn't think he'd like it either. You take it, Lorrie. Do you good to get out. You're too young to stick at home as much as you do. If you could find one of the men teachers at school to go with you, you could have the other ticket, too.'

At first, Lorraine was going to refuse, telling herself that she had too much pride to push herself in where she wasn't wanted. But something made her hesitate. Why shouldn't she accept the ticket?

'D'you know, Mum, I think I will. I'd have to buy something new to wear.'

Beryl's eyes shone. 'I'm so glad, dear. It'll be such a nice change for you.'

Later, her mother went out. Lorraine felt tired and decided to go to bed early and sit up and read. She had taken off her housecoat and was removing her furry mules when there was a tap on the door. She thought, 'Mother's back early,' and called out 'Come in.'

Alan put his head round the door. 'In bed yet? Ah no.' The rest of him followed his head and he wandered in.

Lorraine, thoroughly confused, seized her housecoat and flung it round her shoulders like a cape. 'What have you come in for?'

His eyes went to work and she turned as pink as her thin sleeveless nightdress. 'I'm just going to bed,' she said, still belligerent.

'So I see. I don't mind. Go ahead, get in. I only want to talk to you, my pure-minded chaste little maiden.'

Lorraine felt a little silly and sat on the bed. He lowered himself down beside her and his arm lifted and rested across her shoulders. 'All right, don't cower away. Although the setting's ideal and the time of day just right, I have no intention of seducing you'—he looked at her hopefully—'unless you want me to?'

She laughed at his expression and he laughed with her. 'That's better, much better. Now this book,' he lifted it from the bed where he had put it. 'It's another one of mine which I thought might interest you. It's all about newspaper publishing and it's aimed primarily at the school-child.'

Lorraine took it and opened it eagerly. As she flicked through the chapters, she told him, haltingly, because she knew she was submerging her pride and letting him know he had won, how she was slowly changing her teaching methods. She told him how much his other book had helped her.

'This one will, too. Look, this chapter tells them where a newspaper gets its news from, this tells in detail how the paper is put together. They'll learn what a composite thing a paper is, and also that the same story can be told in many different ways, according to the policy of the proprietors and the style which the editor dictates. It teaches them how to judge whether a newspaper is good or bad and so on.'

'This is wonderful. It will make an excellent subject for discussion in class.'

He watched her eagerness indulgently, saying, 'And it

should keep them interested because, after all, newspapers are part of their everyday lives. You could even teach them how to report events with the minimum of words. That's something every reporter has to learn. Many of them don't, though,' he added ruefully, 'which makes a sub-editor's work all the harder, as I well know.' He was silent for a few moments. 'Look, if it will be any help to you, I'll make a few notes which you could use in class. Would you like that?'

The front door opened and closed and Mrs. Ferrers came up the stairs.

'Would you really do that?' Lorraine asked him. 'It would be a wonderful help.'

'Will do,' he nodded, and Beryl called, 'In bed yet, Lorrie?' Her head was pushed round the door and her mouth dropped open. A frown chased across her forehead and Alan saw it and said, 'It's all right, Mrs. Ferrers. I haven't molested your daughter. I did ask her, but she said "no".'

Beryl's face creased into a relieved smile. 'I didn't really think that of you, Alan. I know you too well.'

'Do you?' he said, half to himself. 'I wonder.'

'By the way, Alan,' Beryl went on, 'Lorrie's going to have my ticket for your centenary dance. I didn't somehow think I was cut out for that sort of thing, nor did James. Lorrie's looking forward to it, aren't you, dear?'

Lorraine nodded and Alan removed his arm from her shoulders. He stood up and went to the door.

'I see.' His expression was blank. 'Well, that saves me the trouble of looking for another partner.' She looked down quickly because she knew she had to keep her joy to herself. 'Goodnight, both of you.'

Beryl went out, too, and Lorraine got into bed. But not to sleep, not for a long time. The thought of being Alan's partner at the dance was enough to keep her awake all night.

Lorraine was having trouble with the lay-out of the school magazine. She and Ann struggled with it one lunch-time and they arranged it in a number of different ways.

'It's no good,' Ann sighed. 'It just won't come right somehow. Ask Alan, Lorraine. Show him what we've done and get his advice. He won't mind.'

Lorraine protested at having to ask him such a favour, but Ann was persuasive. 'He can only say "no", Lorraine. He won't eat you!'

So that evening, while Lorraine was working in the dining-room she listened intently for his key in the front door. As soon as she heard it, she seized the bits and pieces of the school magazine and went into the hall.

Alan was holding the door open for Margot, who smiled at Lorraine, an all-embracing if slightly supercilious smile. As usual, Margot's eyes travelled disparagingly the length and breadth of her, then she waved with a gracious sweep-ing movement and preceded Alan up the stairs.

Lorraine tried to hide her disappointment as she turned away, but Alan must have seen it, because he asked her what she wanted. She said it didn't matter.

'Will it keep?' he asked. Lorraine repeated off-handedly that it didn't matter and shut herself in the dining-room.

Margot was still there when Lorraine went to bed. She heard the laughter and the chatter and the records Alan put on. The smell of cigarettes crept out to the landing and it even irritated Lorraine's nostrils as she tried to shut out their noise and get some sleep. She dropped off at last and didn't hear Margot leave.

Alan left the house with Lorraine next morning. Again he asked her why she had wanted him. 'It was nothing,' she shrugged and walked off with her head in the air.

She didn't know why she was annoyed with him. After all, he had every right to invite anyone he liked to his room. Her mother, as his landlady, had put no time limit on how long his guests could stay—all night, if he wished.

73

With that feline thought, Lorraine walked to the bus stop while Alan drew away in his car in the opposite direction.

That evening he caught her in the hall. He grabbed her arm and forced her to a standstill. 'Tell me what you wanted me for.'

She tried to release her arm. 'I told you, it didn't matter. It still doesn't.'

Somehow the prickles were back in both of them. She jerked her arm away and went into the dining-room. He followed her and watched as she started unpacking her briefcase, placing folders and exercise books all over the table. She pulled out the school magazine, looked at him involuntarily and pushed it back. But he was too quick. He had seen her hesitation and pulled her hand away as it hovered protectively over the divided sections of the case. He peered inside and extracted the magazine.

'Now I know,' he said, and flicked through the roughly assembled pages with the articles temporarily glued into position. He smiled, without looking up. 'Not very good, is it?'

'We're not journalists. We're just simple-minded teachers.' His eyebrows rose at her sarcasm. 'We did the best we could.' She sounded sour even to her own ears, and she realised that it was not the best way to approach someone whose help she needed.

'Well?' His question made Lorraine raise her head. He waited, looking at her like an adult trying to instil good manners into a child. 'What do you say?'

She realized at last what he meant and said, like a sulky schoolgirl, 'Please could you help us improve it?'

'That's better,' he said and drew up a chair next to hers.

For the next hour she was the student and he was the teacher. He taught her the basic principles of magazine lay-out, he showed her how a sub-editor worked. He deleted, he rearranged, he shortened where necessary and indicated which stories and articles could be lengthened.

When he had finished, she told him that it promised to be the finest issue of the school magazine they had ever produced. He smiled. 'And you, as editor, will get all the credit! Fine thing, when I've been sitting here doing all the donkey work.'

She laughed. 'Do you want us to put in an acknowledgement to you—as assistant editor?'

He nearly exploded. '*Assistant* editor? Of all the cheek!' But he was laughing too, and when he went out of the room he was muttering, 'Impudent little minx . . .'

Lorraine had bought a handbag in her effort to make herself look less dowdy. She moved the contents of her old much-loved black one into the new brown leather bag. The other teachers admired it at school next day.

Even Hugh had started to take more notice of her. She wondered if he were at a loose end and trying to get back into favour with her. It looked as though Margot had returned to Alan and left Hugh high and dry. Then Lorraine remembered that he would be taking Margot to the centenary ball. It seemed, Lorraine reflected with some envy, that Margot had the ability to keep two men dangling on a piece of string indefinitely.

She was looking forward to an evening alone. Her mother had gone with James to another branch of his business in a town some miles away, and Alan would probably be working late.

As she approached the front door after school that afternoon, she delved into her handbag for the key. She tried again, and again. In the end, she took out the entire contents of the bag. Then she knew she had to face it—the key was not there. It was probably still in her old handbag, tucked away in the centre compartment. She sat on the step and nearly cried at her own stupidity. There she was, shut out of her own house, with the doors locked against her and all the windows tightly closed.

When the irritation began to recede, the need for action became paramount. She groped about in the dark of her mind for an idea, and when the torchlight shone and picked one out, she nearly rejected it for its impossibility. 'Go to Alan's office,' it said. 'Borrow his key.'

Whether she liked it or not, she had to acknowledge that it was, in fact, the only way out of the ridiculous situation. She rang the bell of the house next door and asked permission to use their phone. They agreed readily and she got through to Alan. When he had recovered from his astonishment at hearing her voice, he burst into raucous laughter.

She said indignantly, 'If you think it's so funny, I won't bother you.' She was about to put the receiver down when she heard him say,

'Don't be an ass, of course you can come and get my key. You'll have to get a bus, won't you? It'll take you a good twenty minutes.'

Lorraine rang off. It took her less than the twenty minutes Alan had estimated and when the receptionist in the entrance foyer of the newspaper office informed the news editor of Lorraine's arrival, she was told to go straight up.

'Get a lift to the third floor,' the girl said, 'and it's the first door on the right.'

When Lorraine entered the room, she almost turned and ran, because six pairs of male eyes, including Alan's, swung round simultaneously and fastened on to her like a dog on to a slipper. The room was spacious and bright and full of warmth from the central heating, but judging by the heat generated by those eyes, Lorraine doubted with some asperity if central heating was needed in that room at all.

Confused, she searched the room for Alan, found him and made for him like someone running to shelter from a rainstorm. He pulled up a chair for her, but she remained standing. She wanted the key and to escape from that room

76

with all possible speed. But Alan had other ideas. He was obviously going to make a meal of her and was not intending to let her go until he had licked the plate clean.

'Now,' he said, scratching his head and leaning back in his chair, 'what was it you wanted to see me about?'

'You know very well,' Lorraine said between her teeth, 'the front door key.'

He clicked his fingers. 'Ah yes.' He grinned and pushed his hands into his pockets. 'You haven't asked me for it yet.' Every eye in the room turned towards them. 'Sit down,' he insisted. 'Take it easy. Rest your legs.' He glanced down at them. 'They're—er—worth looking after.'

Lorraine knew that he could see her annoyance but it only seemed to increase his enjoyment. Someone approached and Lorraine sat down, her back rigid. Another man drifted over. A third came and sat cornerwise on Alan's desk.

'What's this?' Alan asked, smiling and looking round at them. 'An interview? A press conference?'

The table was now surrounded by all the males in the room. 'Come on, Alan, introduce us.'

He did so, but it was a one-way introduction. He went round the table and Lorraine didn't catch all the names.

'Friend of yours, Alan?' one of the men asked.

'Latest girl-friend?' another wanted to know.

'Doubt it,' the man next to him whispered. 'Hardly his type.'

'Come on, Alan. Give. All confessions will be regarded as strictly off the record, completely confidential and utterly unprintable.'

'They're bound to be where Alan's concerned. Never the same bird twice running.'

A twitch of annoyance brought Alan's eyebrows together. 'All right, I'll give. This is Miss Lorraine Ferrers, teacher of English in a very respectable, old-fashioned girls' school in the town.'

'Schoolmarm,' said one disgustedly and started to move away.

'She lives in the house I lodge in——' That brought him back.

Five pairs of eyes nearly leapt from five heads. 'You mean you live in the same house——'

'And you're just very good friends.' Their guffaws were loaded with meaning.

'You're so wrong. We're not even *friends*, are we, Miss Ferrers?' They laughed again. 'I tell you, chaps, this one bites.' There was a general rubbing of hands and an urging forward towards her. 'No, I don't mean in the literal sense. Metaphorically speaking. She doesn't think much of journalists.' Low-pitched growls came from five masculine throats.

'Know what she said to me, first day I set foot in her mother's house?'

Lorraine put a hand on his arm. 'No, don't, please . . .'

He smiled wickedly and her agitation only seemed to increase his determination to go on. 'I'll tell you, but when you've heard it, don't assault her. That I won't allow. She said,' he counted on his fingers, 'she said that having a journalist in the house was like having a spy in residence,' there was a horrified murmur, 'as though the place was being "bugged". She said she regarded journalists as the highest-paid *unskilled* workers in the land,' Lorraine held her breath awaiting their retribution, but Alan went on, 'and she also said that reporters "search in life's dustbins for rotting matter which they force down people's throats." '

There came a shout of laughter and instead of the anger Lorraine had expected, there was in the journalists' eyes a certain grudging admiration which astonished her.

'She's not far wrong, you know,' one of them said, and the others turned on him.

Another said, full of disbelief, 'You've got this firebrand living in the same house and you mean to tell us you've never . . .'

'*Never!* We've never even held hands, have we, Miss Ferrers?'

'You're slipping, mate.'

'We're not all lascivious like you, Bill,' Alan said.

'No?' The insinuation was unmistakable. 'Don't tell me you haven't had your moments.'

Alan's eyes began to darken with something like anger. 'That's neither here nor there.' Lorraine noticed that he did not deny the charge. 'Now look, chaps, the lady came to see me, not you.' The note of authority in his voice had the desired effect and the others drifted away. A young girl brought in a tray of tea. 'Got a spare cup, Moira?' Alan asked.

'I'll get one, Mr. Darby.' She was soon back with one which Alan pushed in front of Lorraine. 'Relax. Refresh yourself before you begin your long journey home.'

Lorraine drank it gladly and as she did so, he pulled a piece of paper towards him. 'Draw up your chair,' he said, 'and look at this.'

She did as she was told, grudgingly, and peered over his shoulder.

He grinned. 'I'll give you a lesson in subbing. Read that, then tell me first, if it needs cutting and if so, how you would do it.'

Obediently she read it and covered the last three or four sentences with her palm.

'You'd do that?' he asked. 'Cut off the vital information those lines contain?'

She read it through again. 'Oh yes, they do.'

'Look,' his pencil went to work, 'first, you have to learn to condense. You put in shorter, everyday words—"attired" becomes "wore", "observed" gets changed to "saw", "informed" becomes "told", "endeavoured" is altered to "tried", and so on. Then you cut out the jargon which crept in without the reporter even realising it. You make it

79

understandable, easy to read and inviting. If necessary, you rewrite it completely and duck out of the way when the bloke who wrote it in the first place makes a bee-line for your desk.'

The ten minutes Lorraine spent listening to Alan explaining his work were so interesting she wished secretly that she could stay longer. He saw her looking at her watch.

'All right, I'll take the hint. So you want the front door key?' He removed it from his key ring and put it into her outstretched hand. He pressed his palm over hers and kept it there just a little longer than necessary. Her heart turned inside out. His eyes delved knife-deep into hers. Then, when he spoke, softly, intimately, he rotated the blade cruelly in the wound. 'As long as it's not the key to my heart you're asking for.' He watched her eyes bleed a little just before she lowered her lids.

As she reached the door, a plaintive voice said, 'Aren't you going to say goodbye, Miss Ferrers? We may be carnivorous animals, but we aren't cannibals. We didn't eat you, did we?'

She turned and looked at the speaker. He seemed so like a disappointed little boy that she laughed. She didn't just smile, she laughed and they looked like six happy men basking in an unexpected burst of sunshine.

CHAPTER V

IT was late November and the Press ball was approaching. Lorraine had to contain her mounting excitement. She knew that Alan would be her partner and the thought was bliss.

Her mother went with her to buy something new to wear. She chose a deep red velvet dress which fitted her perfectly. It was sleeveless and had a low rounded neckline. Beryl said her double row of pearls would set it off nicely.

On the way home in the bus, she told Lorraine that James's son would be home from abroad in a few days.

'I didn't even know he had a son,' Lorraine said.

'I'm sure I told you, dear,' her mother protested, but Lorraine knew she had not. 'His name's Matthew.'

'What's he like?'

'I've seen a photo of him and he's nice-looking, fair-haired like his father, round-faced.'

'Married?'

Beryl shook her head. 'James wishes he'd settle down. He thinks he's got a girl, but he's been abroad two or three years, so James is not sure. He's a civil engineer, builds bridges and things overseas.'

Lorraine tried on her dress again when they arrived home, and she was in her mother's room when they heard Alan's car turn into the driveway. Beryl rushed her back to her own bedroom.

'Quick, dear, don't let him see you in the dress till the dance. It'll be a nice surprise.'

Lorraine changed back into her other clothes and arrived on the landing just as Alan reached the top of the stairs. He had a girl with him. It was not Margot. It was someone equally elegant and, if possible, even more supercilious.

Alan didn't give the girl a chance to speak. He bundled her into his room and closed the door.

Another one of his 'flowers', Lorraine thought, sick at heart. The visitor stayed for a long time. They were very quiet. There was no laughter or chatter as there had been when Alan had entertained Margot. Lorraine felt restless and almost ill with misery. She would rather they had rocked the house to its foundations with noise than produce this silence, this ominous, agonising, intimate silence.

Alan was showing the girl out of the door when Lorraine went up to bed. He sprinted up the stairs as she was going into the bathroom.

'Hallo,' he said, and his cheerfulness put her teeth on edge.

She didn't answer, just gave him a scathing look. His eyes opened wide. 'Why, I do believe she's jealous!'

Lorraine turned on him. 'Me, jealous? Why should I be jealous? You don't mean a thing to me, so don't fool yourself that your magnetic charm is infallible. *I'm* not one of your "flowers", remember!'

Lorraine realised then that she had made a basic mistake. She had expected her sarcasm to shrivel him up, but she had forgotten that she was scantily dressed, ready for washing and with only her semi-transparent housecoat coming between her and near-indecency. One quick glance at Alan's face was sufficient to tell her that he was lapping up her appearance like an eager, tail-wagging dog, and the broad grin that underlined his uninhibited interest goaded her even more. She slammed into the bathroom and tried not to notice that she washed her face with tapwater mixed liberally with salt tears.

Next morning he caught her on the way downstairs.

'If you must know,' he said, as though their conversation had never been interrupted, 'we were working.' She flashed her eyes. 'And if you look at me like that, Miss Ferrers, as though you don't believe a word I'm saying, I'll carry you kicking and screaming into my room, lock the door and do to you what you thought I was doing to her.'

Lorraine was surprised and a little frightened by his sudden anger and swept on down the stairs, gathering about her the few bare threads of dignity he had allowed her to keep.

A few evenings later, Beryl told her daughter, 'I've met Matthew.'

'Matthew?' The name failed to register at first.

'James's son. You remember? Well, he's a fine young man, dear. I've invited him here for a meal. With James, of course.' She named a date.

'That's the day after the centenary dance.'

'That's right. Does it matter?'

'Not really. I don't suppose I'll be very late home the night before.'

The day of the dance arrived, although, like a small child, Lorraine had begun to doubt that it ever would. Her mother helped her dress for it. She had just pulled her white lace-edged slip over her head when there was a tap at the bedroom door. Beryl looked surprised.

'It must be Alan.' Before Lorraine could stop her, she had the door open wide and he was standing there, eyeing her. She searched madly for her housecoat, but it was hanging on the back of the door and she would have had to pass in front of Alan to reach it.

He grinned, 'Are you going in that? You'll be a sensation!'

Lorraine snapped, 'What do you want?'

'Just to tell you that Hugh will be calling for you.'

'But—but'—although her hands covered her flushed cheeks, nothing could hide the dismay in her eyes—'I thought you . . .'

'Sorry,' he said, with a shrug, 'Margot changed her mind. She wants me to partner her, so Hugh's taking you. And what the Margots of this world want, they usually get.'

Lorraine uncovered her cheeks and clenched her fists. She let him see her anger now, and she didn't care what he read into it.

'You're very gallant, as I always knew you were,' she spat out. 'You honour your commitments, keep your promises as nobly as the rest of your kind.'

'Anyone would think,' he drawled as he hooded his eyes and made the most of her state of undress, 'that you were disappointed.'

Beryl, who had been looking from one to the other in some agitation, intervened and Lorraine felt like shaking her. 'Oh, she is, Alan. She's been looking forward to you taking her ever since I gave her the ticket.'

In her fury, Lorraine turned on her mother. 'That's not true,' she cried. 'I've been dreading him as a partner. I'd rather not have gone, really, especially when you told me he would be taking me.'

Her mother opened her mouth. She tried to speak, but nothing came out.

'Is that so?' Alan was addressing Lorraine. 'You tempt me to phone Margot and tell her I'm taking you after all, just to annoy you.'

Beryl forced out a laugh, trying to normalise the situation. 'Well, it doesn't matter really, does it, dear, as long as someone takes you?'

Alan half turned to go out. 'Goodbye, Mrs. Ferrers.' He raised a taunting eyebrow at Lorraine. 'See you later, perhaps?'

When the front door closed on him, Lorraine sat on the bed. 'I don't want to go,' she said, and knew she was being childish.

'What's the matter with you, Lorrie?' Her mother's tearful concern brought her to her senses.

'Sorry, Mum. I didn't mean to snap your head off, but——'

'But you're disappointed, dear? Never mind, you'll see

Alan there, won't you? You might even get the chance of dancing with him,' she added, as though she was offering a child a sweet to 'make it better'.

Lorraine put on her dress and looked at her reflection. She felt let down beyond words. 'It's not Hugh I want,' she thought, 'and I don't suppose he wants me.' She smiled grimly. That made two of them fed up with their partners, two of them looking out for another person. Well, at least they would have something in common!

'That's lovely, dear. It makes you look beautiful, Lorrie.'

Beryl's compliments were laced more strongly with superlatives as the minutes passed. Lorraine knew it was her mother's way of trying to make her feel reconciled to the situation, but it didn't succeed.

She looked at her hair and grew defiant. She borrowed a deep red chiffon scarf from her mother, gathered her hair behind her neck and tied it back.

'Why have you done that?' Beryl asked, and her mother's disappointment almost made her change her mind. 'It looks much nicer loose.'

'Oh, it gets in my way hanging down.' Beryl gave up with a shrug.

Lorraine greeted Hugh with her customary deadpan expression. 'He seems to bring out the blankness in me,' she thought, putting a smile on her face. He seemed to have the effect of anaesthetising her brain and numbing her thoughts so that all she could find to say to him were trivialities and empty phrases.

'Hallo, Lorraine. You look nice.' Even his voice lacked conviction when he talked to her, Lorraine noticed. She supposed she brought out the worst in him, too.

They drove to the hotel on the other side of the town. The car park was filling fast, and they parked near a large cream-coloured car which Lorraine recognised as Alan's. She pulled her coat tightly round her as she waited for Hugh and he took her by the elbow and guided her up the steps into the entrance foyer. He indicated the ladies' cloakroom. 'Meet you here again in a few minutes,' he said.

Lorraine had to push her way through lines of women to reach the mirror. She had thought her dress was good when she was at home with her mother's praise to flatter her, but when she looked at the fabulous dresses some of the others were wearing, she felt almost dowdy.

'Hallo, Miss Ferrers,' It was, of course, Margot, looking radiant and irresistible in white lace and white shoes and a small white flower in her hair.

'Good evening, Miss French.'

'Hugh here?' Margot was eyeing her with casual interest, and the absence of distaste in her look gave Lorraine's self-confidence a small but noticeable boost.

'He's waiting for me in the foyer.'

'Oh well, I must go and find Alan. He's a darling. He said he didn't mind in the least swopping partners at the last minute. He's such a good dancer, and when Hugh told me he wasn't very keen on dancing—well, I just had to have Alan, and you would have to have Hugh. You didn't mind, Miss Ferrers?'

Margot's artless and rather childish anxiety made Lorraine feel a hundred years old. She smiled and shook her head, knowing that was all she could do. She followed Margot into the foyer and saw her wave to Hugh before pushing through the swing doors into the ballroom.

Hugh started to follow her, but checked himself when he saw Lorraine approaching. 'He's no actor,' Lorraine reflected, 'he can't hide his disappointment like I can.'

He took her by the elbow and propelled her quickly into the ballroom. She knew he was hoping to find Margot and Alan and join them, but they were in the centre of a group of their colleagues. They were sitting at a large round table at the side of the hall and they all seemed to be rocking back with laughter at something Margot had said. 'No one should have everything Margot's got,' Lorraine thought savagely. As Hugh found her a seat at a small table, she watched Alan lean forward and gaze into Margot's face. He spoke to her and everyone around them laughed again. Lorraine realised then that Margot was surrounded by men.

A wave of jealousy such as she had never experienced in her life before had her by the throat and nearly choked her. She had to throw off its stranglehold somehow, so she turned to smile at Hugh. But he too was gazing, like a dog about to be left alone in a house, at the girl across the room.

'Is there—is there anything to drink, Hugh?'

He looked guilty at having to be reminded of his duties as escort and apologised immediately. He left her to get the drinks. As she sat alone, waiting, among those crowds, Alan's eyes flickered towards her. They were expressionless and cool and the disinterest in them made her feel as desired as a discarded doll.

She looked around. Could she get away, she wondered, before Hugh returned? She was sure he would not miss her. He would simply drift across the room to Margot, like all the others. But Hugh came back and placed the sherry in front of her. She thanked him with a smile he didn't even see. He took a cigarette from the packet with elaborate care as if to occupy as much time as possible, and settled back to smoke it. The music began and they watched Alan lead Margot on to the dance floor.

Lorraine sensed a tightening in Hugh as he watched them close up until there was barely sufficient room for a sheet of newspaper between them. They seemed to glide to the music in a unity of movement which was perfection.

Lorraine watched them with a feeling of helplessness, knowing that against such odds her battle had been lost before it had even begun.

'Dance, Lorraine?' Hugh's voice was heavy and dutiful.

He took her arm as they moved among the couples already dancing. Lorraine's sense of rhythm was poor and although she knew how to perform the steps, her feet were clumsy and disobedient and she tripped against Hugh so many times their sporadic conversation became punctuated with monotonous words of apology. Hugh tried to laugh it off, but she knew that his tolerance was strained to its limits.

They returned to their table and Hugh stretched out his legs with obvious relief. 'Another drink?' he asked, looking about him as if seeking an escape route.

'No, thanks, Hugh,' Lorraine said, 'but get yourself one. Don't worry about me.'

He went at once and she was alone again. He was away so long, she began to wonder what had happened to him. She glanced at the bar, but he was not there. She looked across to Alan's table and saw a man bending over the back of Margot's chair. It was Hugh. He had a glass in his hand and he was laughing at something she had said.

'High and dry,' Lorraine thought. 'I'm left high and dry.' The words rang stupidly and pointlessly like a doorbell in an empty house. Now she would go, while no one was looking. There was the door marked 'Exit'. She groped at her feet for her handbag and stood up.

A man broke away from a group and lurched towards her. He was tall, except that his shoulders were bent with too much drink. He was young, except that his eyes were glazed and old-looking. He drew up a chair and sat down next to her. His hand was unsteady as he lowered his glass to the table-top. Lorraine tried to get past him, but he caught her hand and pulled her back. In an effort to humour him, she flopped into the chair again.

His words were slurred as he said, 'Now what's a pretty little thing like you doing all alone? Can I get you a drink, dear?'

Before she could reply, another man loped across the

floor. 'If there's anything being given away here, Bill, count me in on it, pal.' He drew his chair up to her other side.

She panicked and gazed round the hall, seeing nothing but a blur of nebulous colour. The man called Bill put his hand over hers, which were clenched together on the table.

'Dance with me, darling?' He started to pull her to her feet, but the other man protested,

'Give me a chance, mate. I'm not so long in the tooth as you are. The lady might prefer me,' and he pulled her the other way. She dragged her arms away from both of them and sat down.

Someone put his arms round her neck and clasped his hands so tightly under her chin that her head was forced back to look up at him. 'Leave this girl alone, you pack of wolves,' Alan said. 'Hands off this one.'

A group was gathering now, and Alan's linked hands loosened slightly.

'Why, boy?' someone asked. 'Is she your property?'

The man called Bill said, 'She must be his latest woman.'

'No, she's not his type,' another said derisively. 'Not flashy enough.'

'Hey, look, mate,' Bill said, 'you've annoyed him now.'

'Get up, Lorraine,' Alan snapped, his eyes dangerous.

She stood up and her heart turned over at his use of her first name. His arm went round her shoulders.

Someone sang, 'Do not trust him, gentle maiden . . .'

Alan said, pointedly, 'Come away from these loud-mouthed lechers.'

He propelled her towards the dance floor, but she resisted. 'Thanks for your rescue act,' she said, more sourly than she had intended, 'but I don't want to dance.'

'Too bad. You're going to dance.'

Still she held back. 'I can't. I'm awful at it. Ask Hugh.'

He jerked her against him. '*Dance*,' he hissed, and after a few moments, miraculously, she did. Whenever she made a mistake he would correct her by gentle pressure from his body. She was so happy, she did not want to talk, but he said, 'Go on, say it.'

'Say what?'

'What you've said since the moment I met you. That journalists are a lot of unethical, sex-crazed drunkards.'

'You've said it for me,' she answered, and saw his lips draw into a thin line.

Still they danced and when the music came to an end, he held her until it started again. She had stopped thinking. She was in a state of suspended time, thought and feeling.

He gatecrashed her reverie. He tightened his hold and said in her ear, 'I've said it before and I'll say it again, you're a first-class little——'

She pulled away and cut him off, 'Now what have I done?'

He lifted a hand and tugged at the hair resting against her neck, but she twisted her head away. 'You put this on to annoy me, didn't you?'

'Yes,' she breathed, bracing herself against the increased pressure of his fingers. 'It's a chiffon scarf and it belongs to my mother.'

'Meaning "hands off"?'

'Certainly.'

The lights were lowered, the atmosphere became intimate, the music persuasively tender. 'Hands off the wearer, too, I suppose that means?' he whispered.

'It certainly does,' she whispered back.

His mouth came down so brutally on hers that she whimpered with pain. He raised his head and laughed. She strained away from him, determined to release herself, but he was equally determined to keep her there. The lights came up, the music ended and it was as if nothing had happened—except that Lorraine was shaking and her cheeks were on fire.

'I'm going home,' she snapped.

'You can't,' he said. 'There are still the speeches and the toasts to come. If you go now, it will be extremely impolite.'

He led her back to the table, thanked her with an exaggerated bow and left her.

Hugh returned soon afterwards with a glass in his hand. He put it in front of her. 'Alan said you needed this. He said he sent it with his love.' Hugh smiled. 'He didn't mean it, of course.' He sat down.

The drink stayed in front of her, untouched. But when the speeches were made and the toasts proposed, she had to drink it. It tasted to her little better than poison.

After the handshaking and the congratulations and the mutual pattings on the backs of the proprietors and editors, circulating and advertising managers, right down to the longest-serving tea lady, the dancing went on. The atmosphere was warming up and the twisting and the sinuous movements of the younger set were catching on. Even the older guests were forsaking their orthodox ballroom dancing and joining in.

Alan stood, and by his actions Lorraine could see he was inviting Margot to do likewise. She remained seated and turned poutingly from him—her movement was calculatedly provocative—and searched the hall. It seemed she was looking for Hugh who was, of course, looking at her. She beckoned and he excused himself from Lorraine and went, like a well-trained domestic animal, to her side.

Alan sauntered round the hall and Lorraine felt an odd tug inside her. She was sure he was making for her. She grabbed her handbag when he was a few feet away and started towards the swing doors, but Alan had anticipated her action and was there before her. His hand shot out and gripped her arm.

'Running away?' he asked, his tone too smooth to trust. 'Come and join in the fun.'

'I don't know how,' she ground out through her teeth.

'I'm only a schoolmarm, remember.'

'In that dress,' he was moving her towards the dancers, 'and with that figure,' they arrived on the floor, 'you'd hardly guess.' He put her firmly opposite him. 'Now, do as the others are doing.' She watched them and tried. It was a futile effort. 'For God's sake,' he said, and only Lorraine could hear him above the din, 'don't be so inhibited.'

She watched him then and he watched her, and it might have been the look in his eyes or the sight of the others years older than herself enjoying themselves in an almost abandoned fashion, but suddenly she found she could do it.

'That's fine,' he encouraged. She tried harder. 'You're good,' he said. He moved nearer. 'In fact, you're devastating.'

Lorraine knew he was being cynical, but she felt growing inside her a response to the twisting movements of his body which, as she moved with him to the hypnotic beat of the music, became almost more than she could bear.

The dancing stopped, the others moved away, but she was aware only of the overpowering masculinity of the man who had partnered her. It was a feeling so new, so enormous in its implications that it left her limp and wilting. He put his arm round her waist, raised his other hand to turn her face to his and held her eyes all the way back to the table.

Hugh and Margot were there and by the time Alan sat her in a chair—her legs felt too weak to support her and she was sure he knew it—she was aware of the devastating fact that, crazy though it was, she was so in love with the man she thought she hated that it was like a physical and unbearable pain. But she also knew that she was more gloriously alive than she had ever been in the whole twenty-six sheltered years of her life.

'Margot,' she heard Alan saying, 'we've swopped partners. Any objections?'

A shaft of anger sped, arrow-swift, through Margot's eyes, but she smiled and stretched her pink-tipped pointed nails in Hugh's direction.

'None at all, darling,' she said. 'Hugh's mine now, aren't you, Hugh? Alan's got to learn he's not the only pebble on the beach. Besides,' she whispered loudly in Lorraine's ear, 'I can get him back any time I want. Until then, Miss Ferrers, I'll lend him to you.' She softened her voice until it had a purring quality and slewed her almond-shaped eyes across to Alan. 'I know he'll be *quite* safe with you, Miss Ferrers.'

Alan raised a cynical eyebrow, smiled and inspected the lines on the palm of his hand as though he were trying to read the future in them. 'I—er—shouldn't be too sure of that, Margot. And for your information,' he abandoned his palm-reading and held Margot's gaze with eyes that were oddly cold, 'I'm not an object to be lent or borrowed. I belong to myself. I'm no one's possession.'

Lorraine admired Alan's efforts to struggle free of Margot's claws, but she knew he was fighting a losing battle. As he had said earlier that evening, 'What the Margots of this world want they usually get.'

Margot stood angrily and pulled Hugh to the dance floor. Alan watched them go and a satisfied smile touched his mouth. The music was low and sweet now, the compelling beat muted into softness. 'Drink, Lorraine?'

She nodded. He whispered in her ear as he passed to go to the bar, 'The name's Alan.' He was soon back and put a glass in front of her.

'Thank you—Alan.' His name tasted like honey on her lips and his smile knocked her heart sideways.

He tossed the last of his drink down his throat. Lorraine sipped hers. He seemed to be growing impatient.

'Get that liquid down you. I want to dance.'

She did as she was told and he took her hand, pulling her behind him. They danced, they were silent and Lorraine was glad. Their bodies moved in perfect unity and he murmured, 'So you can't dance, eh?'

'It's odd,' she replied, 'but with you, I can.'

His smile was deep with a knowledge that was beyond her. They returned to the table and were alone. She tried desperately to suppress a yawn, but it crept up on her like the traitor that it was, and gave away her tiredness.

Alan saw it. 'Tired?'

'I think I must be.'

'But like a child at a party, you don't want to give in.'

She smiled. 'Perhaps.'

'You've enjoyed it?'

'Wonderful, thanks.' She had forgotten the early lonely part of the evening.

'Shall I take you home?'

She was about to shake her head, but it turned into a nod. 'Please, Alan.'

She found her coat in the cloakroom and soon they were in Alan's car, driving through the dark deserted streets. He turned into the driveway, switched off the ignition and there was silence. Every nerve in her body was straining in awareness of him. He took her chin in his fingers, turned her head. Her heart was going mad.

His hand went to the bow at the back of her neck. She felt him loosen it and her hair swung forward. The scarf fell to the floor. Slowly, deliberately, he unbuttoned her coat—one button, two buttons, three.

His hands slipped inside to the small of her back, pressing her forward. Then she was in his arms and his mouth was taking all the strength from her. She was sinking down and down into that uncharted sea and she was drowning in him. After endless minutes he started to pull away, but she found herself clinging to his lips as a drowning man holds fast to a life-raft. Down she went again as his mouth came back harder still on hers. As his hands moved over her, she rejoiced in an ecstasy she had never known before and she never wanted it to end.

When at last it was over, they drew apart and sat in stunned silence.

'My God,' she heard him whisper. 'My *God!*'

She was shattered. She moved away from him and her head flopped back to rest on the upholstered seat. The silence was unbearable. He did not attempt to touch her. As her senses groped back to normality, embarrassment intruded into her consciousness—embarrassment that she had given away to him, uncaring as he was, the strength of her feelings, and embarrassment at his unmistakable discomfiture at her unexpectedly passionate response.

It came to her then what had happened. She had flagrantly trespassed into the place where once he had said he would never allow her to go. She forced her lips to mouth the words she had to speak.

'I'm sorry,' she said dully, and her voice sounded strange, 'to have strayed into your garden.' Bitterness made her pronounce the words clearly now. 'I've grown a bit and I've bloomed a bit under your expert cultivation, haven't I? And now all that's left is for you to pluck me out and throw me away, like the weed I am.' She struggled with the door handle. 'Well, I'm going to save you the trouble.' Her voice faltered and cracked. 'I'm going back, out of the little gate and I'm locking it behind me. Rest assured, I'll never stray into your garden again.'

She got out, shut the car door. 'Thank you for the lift.' She wished desperately she could stop the tremble in her voice. 'Goodnight.'

'Goodnight, Lorraine.' His voice was quiet and controlled. His hand reached for the ignition key, the engine sprang to life, he reversed out of the drive and was gone into the darkness.

CHAPTER VI

LORRAINE lay awake for hours. She thought that Alan must have gone back to the dance, because it was three o'clock before he returned home. When she heard him close his bedroom door, she settled down to sleep at last.

Next morning she felt grim. She dosed herself with tablets. She had to pull herself together fast because, with visitors coming, she would have to give her mother all the help she needed.

Her mother saw her pale face but made no comment. They dusted and cleaned and cooked the food. Lorraine was glad to have something for her hands to do. She had avoided Alan the whole morning and she wondered if he was keeping out of her way, too.

During the afternoon, she went upstairs to dress.

'You'll put on a bit of make-up, won't you, dear?' Beryl had said. 'Wear something pretty. I do want you to look nice.'

Lorraine did not want to let her mother down. She put on a dark blue finely woven tweed dress which she had bought in the shopping spree a few weeks before. She had her own cosmetics now, having decided that it wasn't fair to her mother to keep borrowing hers. She used eye-shadow and mascara, she let her hair hang loose and stood back to look at her reflection. There was a subtle difference about her, a new awareness in her eyes which strangely frightened her, because she knew why it was there.

She met Alan on the landing. His hair was awry, his tie had been loosened at the neck and he looked as if he hadn't shaved. Gone was the immaculate look she had come to expect. 'If my heart is in my eyes,' she thought, as she glanced at him, 'then it's not for want of trying to keep it in

its place.'

They did not smile. They stared wordlessly at each other. His face was serious, his expression unreadable.

'Hallo, Lorraine,' he said.

'Hallo, Alan.'

She had to pass him to reach the stairs and in doing so, their hands brushed. She felt him move and she stiffened, but he had merely stepped back to let her pass. Absurdly disappointed, she went down the stairs.

Her mother met her at the bottom and looked past her up to Alan, who must have been standing there all the time.

Beryl called, 'James is coming to tea, Alan, and he's bringing his son, Matthew. I do want you to meet them. Will you join us for a meal?'

'That's very kind of you, Mrs. Ferrers,' he replied, 'I'd love to meet them, but I won't come to tea, thanks all the same.'

'Well, if you'd rather not . . .' She sounded disappointed. 'But come down anyway and meet them while they're here, won't you?'

She went into the kitchen and Lorraine followed. Her mother eyed her approvingly.

'You look pretty good, too, Mum,' she said. 'You seem so happy. Is there—a special reason?'

'How did you guess, Lorrie? James proposed yesterday.'

'And you accepted?'

Her mother nodded. 'Do you mind, Lorrie?'

Lorraine's eyes filled with tears and she put her arms round her mother. 'Mind, Mum? I'm delighted. Anyway, I've been expecting it.'

Beryl was crying a little and she dabbed at her eyes.

'So it's a sort of celebration tonight?'

Her mother nodded. 'James so wanted Matthew to be here, just like I wanted you here, too—the four of us together.'

'So I'm going to meet my stepbrother-to-be,' Somehow

97

Lorraine's heart lifted. 'I've always wanted a brother. Now I'm going to get one!'

They laughed together, each glad in their own way, until Lorraine thought of the man upstairs.

Beryl opened the door to her visitors. James stood there, smiling, easy, radiating warmth, his arms outstretched, and as Beryl went into them, he hugged her and smiled at Lorraine over her shoulder.

Beside him stood his son, taller than he was, well-built, his hair a thick mop which fell, in an unruly wave, over his forehead. Like his father he had smiling eyes and an easy manner.

The front door was closed, the introductions were made and Lorraine found her hand resting in Mathew's.

'So,' he said, 'after thirty-odd years, I'm acquiring a sister.' He frowned, pretending to be worried. 'You won't fight me and bite me like other brothers' sisters, will you, Lorraine?'

They all laughed, but his father said, 'Don't be daft, lad, she's as much your sister as our next-door neighbour's daughter.'

'That's true, I suppose, but,' he didn't hide the appreciation in his eyes, 'that could have its advantages.'

'Now, now, lad,' James said, a little sharply, 'don't rush your fences.'

They went into the lounge and Beryl sat on the couch. She patted the cushion beside her, looking at James, and he needed no further invitation.

Lorraine stood up. 'Cup of tea?' she asked, her eyes going from one to the other.

'Would you be a dear, Lorrie? And ask Alan if he'd like one, dear,' Beryl called out to her as she went into the hall, 'and remind him he promised to come down and meet James and Matthew later.'

Then Lorraine heard her explaining to Matthew that they had a paying guest, a nice young man he was, a journalist . . .

Lorraine switched on the kettle and when it boiled she decided to make tea for five and take a cup to Alan without asking him first. That way she would only have to see him once.

She tapped on his door, her heart knocking queerly, and when he opened it his face seemed tired and his expression withdrawn. 'Thank you,' he said, taking the tea from her. 'Your visitors have come?'

'Yes,' she answered, her face as blank as his.

'Mother says don't forget to come down and meet them later.'

He nodded briefly. 'Thanks.' He closed the door as she stood there and she felt disproportionately hurt by his action.

She went downstairs and took the tray into the lounge. They chatted and laughed as they drank their tea and afterwards Lorraine slipped out and shut herself in the kitchen to put the finishing touches to the meal. She called to the others, carried the food to the dining-room and served the guests, helped by her mother who had insisted on taking up her role of hostess.

Lorraine made the coffee and they drank it in the lounge. Beryl said, 'I'm sure Alan would like a cup. I'll call him.'

He came in, tidy now, his tie straight and his thick dark hair fresh from combing. First he shook James by the hand, then Matthew, and the two of them stood talking by the fireplace.

'Give Alan some coffee, Lorrie,' Beryl whispered.

He accepted the cup Lorraine offered him and spooned in the sugar. He thanked her and their eyes met and held. She tried to read his expression but failed. Her pulses racing, she turned away, making for the armchair like a child running to the comfort of its mother's arms. Alan drank his coffee, still talking to Matthew, while Beryl and James held hands on the couch.

Then they told Alan their news and he said he wasn't really surprised. He had been expecting it. Matthew laughed and said that was his 'news sense' coming out.

'Professional journalists, they're all the same,' he joked. 'They put two and two together and make five. Only this time you got your sums right.'

Alan laughed at the joke against himself, drew Beryl towards him and kissed her on the cheek, then he turned to James and shook his hand. James, in turn, kissed Beryl.

'Let's all join in,' said Matthew, and kissed Beryl, then he went towards Lorraine. He pulled her out of the armchair. 'Do you mind, little sister, if I kiss you?'

He bent his head and touched her cheek with his lips. 'Very brotherly,' he said, 'very circumspect. Come on, Alan, quick, while the lady's willing.'

Lorraine backed away. 'No,' she said, 'it doesn't matter. Really it doesn't.'

Matthew laughed. 'The young lady's shy. Don't let that put you off, Alan. The shy ones are best. You know what they say about still waters.'

Alan strolled across to her. 'Why not, indeed? If this is a free-for-all, I certainly don't want to be left out.' He gripped her elbows and drew her towards him. She resisted. He smiled. 'Shy, Lorraine?' There was a wealth of meaning in his question. 'Of *me*? Surely not.'

With the others looking on, she had to submit. His lips pressed against hers, so warm, so gentle and so different from last night. It was agony and it was heaven and it was quickly over. As he drew away, he smiled without releasing her. 'Anyone would think,' there was mockery and wicked amusement in his voice, 'that you'd never been kissed before.'

The others laughed and he let her go. She sank into the armchair. Desperate to remove their attention from her, she asked, 'When is it to be, Mum?'

'Oh,' James said vaguely, 'two or three months, when

we've brought some order to our affairs.' Beryl nodded.

'By the way,' Alan said, walking across to Lorraine, and pulling something from his pocket, 'I found this in my car. Yours, I believe?' He raised an eyebrow.

Lorraine glared at him. 'He knows perfectly well it's mine,' she thought. She took it without thanking him.

'Oh yes,' Beryl said, 'that's the scarf you borrowed from me to wear last night, Lorrie. How did it get in Alan's car?'

Lorraine stuffed it behind a cushion and turned angry eyes on the man in front of her. He was smiling. She stumbled over her words. 'It—it must have—somehow—fallen off when Alan brought me home from the dance.'

She saw Matthew's eyes dart inquiringly from her to Alan and back and wondered how much he had concluded from her pink cheeks and Alan's reminiscent half smile. Matthew moved to her side and sat on the arm of her chair, while Alan propped himself against the wall.

'The trouble with Lorrie is,' Beryl said, determined, to her daughter's annoyance, to keep her in the limelight, 'she doesn't go out enough. She works in that stuffy old school during the day, comes home and works again at night. It's not right when she's so young.'

Matthew looked down at her. 'What, no boy-friend, Lorraine?'

She wished Alan would turn off his lazy smile. 'I—I did have one, but we agreed to part. It didn't work out some-how.'

'So the field's clear? Now, since I'm between girl-friends——'

'I thought you had one, son?'

'I did, but when she heard I was returning to England and leaving her behind, she as good as told me to go to blazes. So,' he turned back to Lorraine, 'I offer you myself with a cracked but not broken heart, to act as escort and substitute boy-friend, and I'll be delighted to take you around.'

Alan moved abruptly. He glanced at his watch. 'I must be off. I have a date.' He looked at Beryl. 'Will you excuse me?'

James laughed. 'What's she like, Alan? Blonde, brunette, redhead?'

'Well now,' Alan's expression became dreamy, 'she's superb to look at, she has beautiful auburn hair and she's everything a man could wish for.' His eyes flicked Lorraine like a whip. 'And her name's Margot.' He raised his hand and left them.

The coming of Matthew brought a new era into Lorraine's life. He kept his word and they went to places she thought she would never go to. He took her to shows, to dances, for drives in the country on sunny winter Sundays. They dined at out-of-the-way hotels with secluded alcoves and subdued lighting. They even sat at home together watching television or just reading.

She thanked him one evening for being so good to her. They were sitting on the couch and had just switched off the television after a particularly moving play.

'An attractive young woman need never thank a man for his company, Lorraine. It should be the other way round. He gets pleasure from being with her. Anyway,' he grasped her arm and somehow manoeuvred her on to his knee, 'hasn't it occurred to you why I may be doing it?'

She held herself stiff and away from him. She shook her head.

'Hasn't it occurred to you,' he went on, 'that I might have fallen in love with you?'

Again she shook her head, more vigorously this time, 'I'm not the type to have that effect on a man.'

'Fishing for compliments, eh?'

'No, just speaking the truth. I know my own limitations.'

He laughed as though what she had said was really funny. 'You don't, you know. You don't know yourself at all, little sister.'

Lorraine pulled away.

'I'm sorry. In the circumstances, that expression was bungling and quite inappropriate. I'll substitute "love" for sister. Is that better?'

'Worse still,' she answered, smiling.

'Oh dear.' He looked puzzled. 'Lorraine, I want to kiss you, but it won't be a brotherly kiss. Do you mind?'

Before she could answer he was kissing her, but she didn't like it at all. She went rigid and tried to pull away and when he had finished he looked so disappointed Lorraine could not forgive herself. She wanted to apologise and tell him, 'I love a man so much I can't bear any other man to touch me.'

There was a tap at the door and Matthew called, 'Come in.'

The newcomer stopped and stared and started to withdraw. Matthew turned his head and Lorraine struggled to stand up, but he held her fast. 'Who's that? Oh, Alan, come in.'

'It can wait,' he said curtly. 'Sorry I disturbed you.'

'No, no, you're not disturbing anything, old chap. Come in, sit down.' Alan remained standing. 'There's nothing doing here, Alan,' Matthew told him. 'I've tried, but it's no use. This girl's a lump of ice. Stone-cold to the core.'

Lorraine caught Alan's falsely incredulous smile and wanted to hit him. 'Lorraine cold, Matthew? You really surprise me. But then I always did think that women schoolteachers were——'

Lorraine cut in, her eyes violent, 'Dull, too respectable for words and——'

'And *very* unexciting,' he finished, his voice soft with malice.

'So now you know,' she said to Matthew, trying to edge

off his knee.

'Ah, but do I?' he persisted. 'What about you having a try, Alan?' He pretended to hand her over. 'Have a go. You might get a warmer response.'

She shrank back against Matthew's chest and his arms went round her. 'My word,' he said, looking delighted. 'I try to get rid of her to another man, and she clings to me tighter than ever. There must be a moral in that somewhere!'

Trapped between two laughing men, she wrenched herself upright. She stood and scowled at Alan. 'Did you want something?'

'I did.' His voice reprimanded her for her bad temper. 'But it will have to wait.'

She asked sulkily, 'Why?'

'Why? Because the person I wish to see appears to be out. In other words, your mother.' She hated his tone which was still rebuking her and it rankled so much, it drove her on.

'Won't I do?'

'No, Miss Ferrers, you won't do.' He spoke so quietly she began to feel ashamed.

'I'm sorry,' she turned away to hide the colour in her cheeks, 'I was only trying to help.'

She realised then what an interested spectator Matthew had been. Alan went away and Matthew left soon after that.

When Beryl came home, Lorraine was in the kitchen, and as they talked, they heard Alan come down the stairs.

He was holding a letter. 'From my mother,' he said.

'And how's Nancy?' Beryl asked eagerly.

'She's fine, apparently. She's asking about Christmas. She wants to know if I'll be going home then. I've arranged to take three days off.' He hesitated. 'You'd have no objection if I went?' He looked straight at Beryl and Lorraine was glad because if he had looked at her, he would have

104

seen her disappointment.

'Objection, Alan? None at all, my dear.' She laughed. 'Your room will still be there when you come back.'

'That's another thing—you'll give me good notice of when you want me to move out, won't you?' They both looked at him sharply.

'Move out?' Beryl asked. 'You mean when I marry James?' He nodded. 'Oh, you've no need to bother your head about that yet, Alan. Why, even Lorrie here, my own daughter, has asked me that stupid question. When will I want her to go? she wanted to know.'

Lorraine met the query in Alan's eyes, but she gave him no answer.

Beryl was talking. 'I'd love to see your mother again, to talk over old times and tell her about James ... You don't think she'd come and stay a couple of nights some time?'

He brightened. 'Ask her. I'm sure she'd like the idea. She dearly loves a good gossip.'

'Go on,' Beryl laughed, 'say it! Like all women. Of course, men never gossip, do they?'

'Of course not,' Alan joked. 'Their minds move on much higher intellectual planes. Talking of that,' he turned to Lorraine and Beryl moved away, 'you may remember that some time ago I promised to make a few notes for you on newspaper organisation? Well, they'll be ready soon. I'll have a chat with you some time and let you have them.'

'That's very kind of you,' Lorraine thanked him stiltedly, trying to keep the pleasure from her voice. 'I'm sure they will be most useful.'

He smiled at her primness. 'I'll sure they will,' he mocked, and returned to his room.

One evening Matthew took Lorraine out to dinner. She was wearing a new pale green suit trimmed with bronze ornamental buttons and she had used her cosmetics with a heavy hand. It was something she often did these days, even for school, hoping perhaps that it would hide from other people the dull ache which had her in its grip and which gnawed at her relentlessly all the time.

It was while they were drinking their coffee that Matthew asked, with studied disinterest, 'Is there a man on your mind?'

She was so taken by surprise that she spluttered and choked. She apologised and dabbed at her watery eyes.

'I think I have my answer,' he remarked, lifting the sugar crystals with a spoon and letting them fall back into the bowl. 'And I think I know who it is.'

He looked up at her quickly for confirmation and she looked down. 'I'm sorry, Matthew.' She fiddled with her spoon, too. 'It's all so useless, because it is, literally, a hopeless case.'

'I only wish I could help you.'

She shrugged. 'You can't change a man's nature. If, as he once told me, he prefers an assortment of women in his life, rather than one steady woman, there's nothing anyone can do, is there?'

'He actually told you that?'

She repeated to him exactly what Alan had said, and he threw back his head and laughed. 'His women are like flowers in a garden, eh?' He laughed again, unbelieving. 'Journalese, my dear. His stock in-trade.'

She shook her head. 'I wish that were true. Anyway, our moralities don't go together. He told me that, too.'

'Meaning?'

'That I'm the faithful type. He's not.'

'M'm.' He looked interested. 'I'd like to know what he was getting at.'

'Don't ask him, Matthew. Please.'

He patted her hand. 'Don't worry, I won't.'

At school, Ann asked her how she was getting along with her stepbrother-to-be. 'Fine,' Lorraine told her. 'He's so nice.'

'Not falling for him? You know, substitute love and all that.'

'Of course not. Matthew's too nice to have that inflicted on him. By the way, would you like to meet him?'

'If he's tall, strong and handsome, the answer's "yes please." '

'He'll be there this evening, so come along about eight.'

'I will,' Ann promised. 'Incidentally, dear,' she eyed her up and down, 'I've said it before, but it will bear repetition—the new you is a distinct improvement on the old.'

'Thanks, Ann. It's mainly due to your encouragement. You're the one who as good as told me to stop looking like a frump.'

'You evidently got the message. Any more—er—results from the person who shall be nameless?'

Lorraine's burning cheeks gave the game away and Ann's interested glance did nothing to put out the fire. Lorraine had not told her about the night of the dance. She had not told anyone. It was a memory she cherished too dearly for that.

'Nothing really to report,' she answered, trying to sound off-hand.

'Now, after raising my hopes beyond belief by your intriguing if silent response, that reply is what might be called "bathos"—in other words, the most maddening anticlimax. Come on, tell Auntie.'

Lorraine shook her head. 'If there were anything to tell, Ann, I would, gladly. Anyway, do come this evening.'

Lorraine had told Matthew that Ann was coming and they both went into the hall to greet her. She looked good in her new fawn winter coat and when Lorraine took it from her, she saw the new red woollen dress underneath.

'Smart, isn't it?' Ann asked. 'Congratulate me on my choice.' Lorraine laughed and did so. 'It's warm, too. It needs to be. It's as cold as the Arctic outside.'

She was introduced to Matthew and shook his hand.

'You feel warm, though,' she commented, smiling at him.

'You're so right,' he laughed, summing her up at once, 'would you like me to prove it?'

She met his banter in her easy good-natured way. She whipped off her glasses and held out her cheek. 'Would you?'

Then Alan appeared on the landing and she raised her hand to him. 'Alan! How nice to see you again. Why did you drop me out of your life?'

'My dear Ann,' he came down the stairs, hands outstretched, 'never let it be said that I treat *you* like I treat all the other women in my life. You're different.'

She took his hands. 'That's what you tell them all, of course.'

He nodded with mock seriousness. 'It's my own special technique, Ann. You've no idea how it flatters their vanity.'

Lorraine clenched her fingers, one by one, into the palms of her hands.

Alan asked, 'Is this a purely private gathering, or——?'

Matthew smiled. 'Lorraine, he's fishing for an invitation. You don't mind if he joins us, do you?'

Before she could reply, Alan said, 'I was going to suggest that you all came up to my room for a drink.'

'Well?' Matthew looked from Lorraine to Ann.

'Suits me,' said Ann.

Lorraine lifted her shoulders carelessly. 'It looks as though everyone else wants to.'

If Alan noticed her reluctance, he didn't show it. 'Come on up. But you'll have to excuse the mess.'

'We see what you mean,' Ann said, walking into the room.

There were papers strewn around the portable typewriter on the table. Newspapers were piled high on the window-sill and floor and even the bed was covered with them like a bizarre quilt.

'You obviously want to create the impression that you're

working really hard,' said Matthew.

Alan laughed. 'Believe it or not, I do work hard sometimes, even though I'm a journalist.' He threw Lorraine a sly look. 'In between entertaining women—in the plural.'

'You know,' Ann said, dropping a pile of papers to the floor and sitting in an armchair, 'I'm sure you're not really the rake you would have us think you are.'

'No?' His eyelids drooped. 'Ask my colleagues.'

'I don't need to,' Lorraine thought miserably. 'I've already heard their comments on the subject.'

'Anyway,' he went on, 'whether I am or not is neither here nor there. It goes with my image.' Again he looked at Lorraine. 'Doesn't it?'

She turned away and moved to sit beside Matthew on the couch. 'Yes,' she answered, as Matthew put his arm round her and drew her close, 'just as dull respectability goes with mine.'

Ann laughed uproariously. 'Judging by the look in Matthew's eye, Lorraine, those are what might be described as "famous last words." Watch out, I'm sure he has designs on your respectability.'

Matthew kissed Lorraine's cheek. 'Now that is an idea.'

'Drink, Matthew?' Alan's tone was so abrupt it brought Lorraine's head up.

'Please, Alan. Sherry, dry, if you have it.'

'Lorraine?' His voice was sharp. 'Medium? Sweet?'

'Oh, sweet, surely?' said Matthew, lolling against her. 'It goes with her image.'

Ann applauded. 'Oh, very good, Matthew.'

'Medium or sweet, Lorraine?' Alan repeated the words slowly, clearly and with some annoyance.

'Sweet, please,' she told him, 'as Matthew said.'

'You see, Alan, I know her taste.' He picked up her hand and played with her fingers. 'You get to know a lot about a girl when you've taken her around as much as I've taken this one.'

'But, Matthew,' Ann said, 'Alan wouldn't know that. He never stays acquainted with a girl long enough to get to know her all that well, do you, Alan?'

'Let's change the subject,' Alan suggested shortly, giving Lorraine a glass, then Ann, and sitting down. 'Women bore me.'

'Talking of men,' Ann went on, with a sideways smile, 'I've noticed at school lately, Lorraine, that Hugh's interest in you seems to be reviving.'

Lorraine looked into her glass. 'You may be right, Ann. He did ask me out one evening, but I turned him down.'

'He must have got over his passion for Margot,' Ann commented. 'Unless she threw him over. Either way, that leaves the field clear for you again, Alan, doesn't it?'

'Oh,' he replied, draining his glass and stretching across to put it on the table, 'Margot's little excursions with other men never worry me. She always returns to the fold.'

Lorraine asked over-sweetly, 'So, despite appearances, she's really the faithful type at heart, is she, Alan? The type who sticks to her man?'

His head shot up and the look he gave her made her reel. 'Yes,' he answered, his eyes slitted and dangerous, 'the faithful type, like you.' The sneer in his voice took the colour from her cheeks.

She was uncomfortably aware that Ann and Matthew were watching them closely. They were alert and vigilant and she frowned, unable to grasp what was going on in their minds. She could not understand the subtle emotional undercurrents which seemed to be pulling first one way then the other.

Ann stood up and wandered over to the record holder standing on the built-in bookshelves. 'I think some music would have a soothing effect on us all. May we, Alan?'

'A record? Certainly, Ann.' He pushed her aside gently and selected one. 'This, I think.'

Ann peered over his shoulder. 'One of my favourites,' she

commented.

Even before Alan put it on the turntable, Lorraine knew what it was going to be and when the haunting tune began and she listened to the words, she remembered the last time she had heard that record. The message came through— '*And I will love thee still, my dear, Till a' the seas gang dry.*' Lorraine flicked open her eyes, daring for a moment to look at Alan. He was staring at her with such concentrated cynicism that she recoiled as if he had thrown acid at her. Quickly she shut him out again.

At last Alan rose to take off the record and Matthew, deeply moved, said, 'A good song. You think so, Lorraine?'

She nodded and he drew her close. She did not resist because she needed at that moment the comfort and reassurance which his action offered her. She could not understand why Alan had chosen to play that piece of music and it seemed to be of immense importance that she should know the answer.

Matthew was whispering against her ear, 'It could be a message from me to you.'

She drew away slightly, rejecting in her mind what he was trying to say. Afraid that Alan had overheard, she glanced at him, but he seemed to be oblivious of everything but the record player. He put on some more music, neutral and calming, and it reduced the emotional temperature in them all.

He produced a box of chocolates which he handed round. He offered a cigarette to Matthew, who refused, took one himself and flicked his lighter to get it going.

The talk became general. Lorraine offered to make some coffee. 'If you wouldn't mind,' Alan said, without looking at her.

Ann went downstairs with her and they made the coffee, found some scones and buttered them, piled cheese biscuits on to a dish and put out a few small cakes which Beryl had baked.

111

They carried the trays upstairs and as Lorraine poured the coffee, Ann handed round the food. Alan went to his bedside table and opened a drawer. He waved some cards in the air. 'Four press tickets going free for a concert next week,' he said. 'Any offers?'

Matthew asked what they were playing.

'Can't remember the whole programme,' Alan told him, 'but the main item is the New World Symphony.' He turned his back on Lorraine and held out two tickets to Matthew. 'Yes?'

'Definitely yes, thanks.' Matthew took the tickets and showed them to Lorraine. 'It's a date?'

She nodded. 'I love the New World.'

Alan said to Ann, 'Shall I keep our tickets?'

She smiled at him brightly. 'Why, am I going with you?'

'I assumed that you were.'

'Delighted. But haven't you anyone more—er—glamorous lined up? Margot, for instance?'

His answer was terse. 'Margot is no music-lover.'

'Then I'd love to go with you, Alan,' she smiled with some significance, 'even if I am only second-best.' He looked at her curiously and her eyes challenged him back. They seemed to be playing some sort of game. 'Are the four seats together?' she asked.

'They are.'

'How do we get there? Do our respective partners call for us?' She looked at Lorraine. 'It seems a bit daft, you and Alan living in the same house, but each going separately.'

'I'll call for you, Ann,' Alan said, curt to the point of rudeness.

'And I'll call for my favourite girl-friend,' said Matthew, resting his hand on Lorraine's knee.

'Then that's settled,' Ann remarked, full of good cheer. 'Thanks for giving us the tickets, Alan.'

He shrugged, threw himself in a chair and drew hard on

his cigarette. Ann flicked through her diary. 'My word it's getting uncomfortably near Christmas. Done all your shopping, Lorraine?'

'Not yet,' Lorraine answered. She looked at Matthew. 'I suppose I'll have to extend my presents list this year, now I've got a stepfather-to-be and a step——'

He grabbed at her hair and she winced. 'If you say the word "brother" I'll brain you, young woman! Boy-friend, if you like, but brother,' he shook his head, 'definitely out.' He released her hair and she rubbed her scalp.

'All right, boy-friend, but I don't know my boy-friend's tastes.'

'I don't know yours, but I'm going to buy you something. Tell me, do you fancy diamonds set in platinum?'

Lorraine's head whirled round. 'All right, calm down.' He patted her hand, amused at her gaping expression. 'Anyone would think I'd just proposed, and that is something I certainly wouldn't do in public. Anyway, as my father advised, I won't rush my fences.'

Ann and Alan were looking on, Ann smiling, Alan silent, with hard narrowed eyes, smoking his third cigarette.

Ann sighed, 'Oh, for a boy-friend who offered me diamonds and platinum!'

They all laughed and relaxed as she had intended them to do. She looked at her watch. 'Sad to say, it's time to go.' She thanked Alan for a pleasant evening and when Matthew offered her a lift, she accepted gladly.

Lorraine went downstairs and waved them off and when she returned to Alan's room, he was collecting the empty cups and stacking them on the tray.

'I'll help you wash these,' he said.

'No, thank you,' she answered in a voice which sounded much cooler than she felt. 'It won't take me long.'

He said, quietly, 'As you wish.'

They both put something on the tray together and their hands made contact. The place where he had touched her

113

seemed to burn and involuntarily her eyes went to his. He was looking at her with an expression which frightened her because of what it did to her. She felt herself swaying towards him.

He made no movement in return. He merely raised his eyebrows in a cool, calculated question. Her cheeks flamed with humiliation and she seized the tray and almost ran from the room. She knew that he would be smiling the smile of the victor at her retreating back.

CHAPTER VII

LORRAINE bought a new dress for the concert. It was black, a shade she rarely chose, with a low neckline and three-quarter sleeves.

'It shows off your graceful neck, dear,' her mother said, with unashamed maternal prejudice, 'and your fair skin, and your lovely figure.'

Lorraine kissed her cheek. 'I take all your motherly compliments with a daughterly pinch of salt, Mum.'

'But it's true. You're a different girl nowadays. You've come out of your shell.'

Lorraine put her hand over her shoulder and patted her back. 'The shell's still there, you know, in case I ever need to go back to it! But it's invisible—no one knows it's there.'

'Yes, dear,' her mother said, humouring her. 'Here are my pearls. They'll look just right on your long neck.'

'If you say much more about my neck,' said Lorraine, taking them and putting them on, 'I'll think I've turned into a swan.'

'Well, in a way you have,' Beryl said. 'You're not an ugly duckling any more. You're beautiful now.'

'Yes, Mum,' Lorraine murmured, humouring her mother now.

'Is Alan taking you?'

'No, Matthew's calling for me. Alan's taking Ann.'

'That's a funny arrangement, with Alan living here.'

'He seemed to want to take Ann.'

'Oh, I see,' she said, but Lorraine knew that she didn't see.

Matthew arrived, kissed Beryl on the cheek and Lorraine on the lips. When he saw her dress, he whistled. 'That'll set them talking,' he said, but he did not specify who 'them'

115

was.

Ann and Alan were waiting in the entrance foyer of the concert hall. The subtle perfume of the hot-house flowers arranged in giant vases around the walls brought tantalising reminders of spring days. The pile of the carpet gave softly beneath the feet and, in spite of herself, Lorraine felt unreasonably happy. In an effort to rationalise her feelings, she told herself that she was, after all, going to spend the next two hours in Alan's company and share with him a piece of music they both loved.

People milled around, some pushing, some allowing themselves to be carried along by the others. Now and then, as they waited for the crowds to clear, Alan raised his hand to friends and acquaintances. He seemed to be popular and one or two men shook his hand and introduced their escorts. He, in turn, introduced his guests to them. Most of his friends were from the newspaper world and he talked shop with them for a few minutes.

At last they filed into their seats, and it seemed to Lorraine that Alan had put himself as far away from her as possible. Matthew and Ann separated them and he was so far away from her as to make any direct communication impossible. If she had had anything to say to him it would have to be channelled through the others, and her expectation of getting pleasure from the evening ebbed away entirely.

She glanced along the row and noticed that, as they studied their programme, Ann's head was almost touching Alan's. She had to suppress a vicious stab of jealousy and at once she felt a sense of guilt. Ann was, after all, her closest friend, although she had to acknowledge that she would have been jealous of anyone, no matter who it was, who happened to be sitting next to Alan at that moment and sharing his programme so intimately.

Matthew drew her arm through his. 'Come out of that day-dream, love,' he said. 'Judging by your expression, it's

116

not a very happy one.'

'Sorry, Matthew,' she whispered.

The orchestra was assembling and Matthew offered her the programme. They read it together, their heads as close as the others. Matthew put his lips to her cheek and Lorraine hoped, with a spark of spite, that Alan was watching. Ann must have been because Lorraine heard her murmur to Alan, 'Look at those two love-birds.' Matthew laughed and did it again.

The first part of the concert was devoted to an overture by Beethoven and works by modern composers. They were well received by the audience and as the interval began, Ann leaned across Matthew and said, 'Alan wants a drink and says what about you?'

Lorraine nodded and they filed out of the auditorium behind the slow-moving crowds. Alan and Matthew fought their way to the bar at the far end of the entrance foyer and returned with the drinks.

Alan greeted some more acquaintances and moved away from the group to talk to two or three attractive, well-groomed young women who seemed to Lorraine to be queueing up for the privilege. She saw with bitter amusement that he dealt with one girl at a time, while the others hung back awaiting their turn.

When he rejoined the others, Ann asked him, 'Members of your harem?'

He laughed uncomfortably and Matthew said, 'Don't ask leading questions, Ann. The answer could be embarrassing.'

'One or two ex-girl-friends, if you must know,' Alan replied, his manner indicating that he did not want the matter discussed.

Lorraine tried to stop herself, but the words came out. She asked, guilelessly, her eyes wide open, 'Some of your plucked-out flowers, Alan?'

Ann seemed puzzled, Matthew threw back his head and laughed and Alan looked as though he would like to throttle her. The warning bell indicated that the end of the interval was near. Lorraine went with Ann to the cloakroom and was puzzled when Ann left her there. She rejoined the others and discovered the reason—her place had been moved along the row so that she was sitting next to Alan while Ann had changed to the seat on the other side of Matthew. Since Alan seemed put out at the new arrangement, Lorraine decided that it must have been Ann's idea.

Alan looked at her in the subdued lighting as though she were something unpleasant that had been left on his doorstep.

Lorraine muttered childishly, 'This wasn't my idea.'

'Nor mine,' he muttered back. He thrust the programme on to her lap. His action told her that there would be no sharing as there had been with Ann, no touching of heads or hands. She bit her lip to keep it still and peered at the programme notes with moist eyes.

The lights were dimmed and she pushed the programme back on to Alan's knees. He took it with bad grace. All the time Ann and Matthew had been talking as serenely as if nothing had happened. This irritated Lorraine beyond words, because she was certain that they were at the bottom of it.

The second half of the concert began. Lorraine made every effort to lose herself in the magnificent music, but the presence of the man on her left acted as a barrier to all rational thought and feeling. She could think of nothing else but that he was there. She started to fidget. She played with her handbag strap. She felt for her gloves, crossed and recrossed her legs.

There was a long-suffering sigh in the vicinity of her left ear, and she took the hint and did her best to sit still. But her hands moved again, this time more agitatedly than ever.

She heard an angry hiss from her left. 'If you don't sit still, woman, I'll—here give me your hand.' He felt for it in the semi-darkness, grasped it and carried it across to his

118

lap. As his fingers closed on hers, he whispered, 'Now, for God's sake keep still and let me listen to the music. If you don't, I'll grab the other hand, too.'

Confused, Lorraine turned her head to see if Matthew was watching, but he seemed oblivious to everything but the music. She tried to pull her hand away, but Alan entwined his fingers round hers even more determinedly. Slowly her tension eased and she relaxed at last. She felt him respond. His muscles slackened and the rigidity left his body.

Now the music sounded sweeter, becoming more poignant with a greater depth of meaning. The grip on her hand loosened and became almost a caress. She could have taken her hand away, but she let it stay where it was. She stole a look at him and at the same moment he turned towards her. They exchanged smiles and for a few ecstatic moments there was peace between them. But Lorraine knew in her heart that it was the effect of the music, nothing more.

When the concert was over they moved, dazed, with the crowds to the doors. They stood in the entrance foyer and the cold air from outside broke into the warmth around them making them shiver in anticipation of the lower temperature outside.

Ann looked at Matthew and said to Lorraine, 'It seems silly for Alan to take me home when you both live at the same house.'

Before Lorraine could reply Matthew said, 'Right, I take Ann, Alan takes Lorraine. Come on, Ann, let's say goodnight and thank you and we'll be off.'

They were moving away through the doors into the darkness before Lorraine had had time to speak a word in protest.

Alan looked at her. 'It seems we're stuck with each other. Too bad if it upsets you.' He took her elbow and manoeuvred her outside.

'It looks as though you are,' she muttered sulkily, and he

gave her a look which was clearly meant to quell her, but she tried to jerk her arm from his.

'Stop behaving like a spoilt, disappointed brat,' he said. 'It's not my fault if your boy-friend decides he prefers another woman's company.'

Lorraine was so surprised at the interpretation he had put on the arrangement which had somehow been forced on them that she walked by his side like an obedient child.

They drove home and while Alan garaged the car, she opened the front door. The house was empty. Her mother got home late sometimes and Lorraine usually had a hot drink ready for her.

She went into the kitchen and put some cups on a tray. Alan stood in the doorway. 'I'm making some cocoa,' she said, her tone as cold as the air outside.

'I could certainly do with something to warm me up,' he remarked, making a pretence of turning up his jacket collar. 'There's a distinct chill in the atmosphere.'

A hint of a smile sidled against his cheek and he leaned against the door and watched her pour the milk into the saucepan. He didn't speak and Lorraine knew that he was still hearing the music in his mind, as she was.

He took the cups into the dining-room and she switched on the electric heater. They drank their cocoa in silence. She was thinking, 'Here's the quiet man again, the man I desperately want to reach, the real person under the cynical veneer, that frightening hard cover of worldliness.'

His voice broke through. 'Did you enjoy the concert?'

'Wonderful, thank you.'

'Despite the fact that I held your hand?' The mocking smile was there again.

'Even in spite of that,' she answered in the same tone.

He looked at his watch, stood up, yawned and stretched. 'Bed, I think.' His eyes dwelt on her and she wondered what was coming.

'Aren't you going to say thank you?'

'You mean for the tickets?'

'Yes, and for bringing you home.'

'Thank you for the tickets and for bringing me home.'

He shook his head. 'Not good enough. I want my money's worth.'

She began to get suspicious as she saw a smile flit across his mouth. 'Don't you know what I mean?' She hesitated to answer, trying to evade the idea that snaked into her mind.

He persisted, 'What does a man usually expect when he brings a girl home?'

'Don't be silly,' she said, feeling absurdly anxious. 'This is different.'

'Is it?' He moved towards her and she moved back. 'I don't agree.'

She inched away again. 'I—I did enjoy the concert,' she remarked conversationally, saying anything that came into her head to distract him.

'You've said that before,' he said, getting nearer.

'The—the orchestra was excellent . . .'

'It was, wasn't it?' Still he pressed on towards her.

She grew afraid of the concentrated look in his eyes. Her heart was banging against her ribs and she continued to edge away, only to find herself backing on to the windows. 'The music was——'

But it was useless. She was caught, breathless, helpless among the curtains, and there was no escape route. His arms fastened round her and she looked up into his face.

He was smiling. 'Come on, I'm waiting.'

But she couldn't do it.

'I'll tell you what,' he said, 'close your eyes, imagine I'm some nasty tasting medicine and get it over quickly.'

She laughed and his arms tightened. Again she hesitated. 'No, better still,' he went on, 'imagine you're kissing Matthew. That should help.'

He bent his head expectantly and she knew she had no alternative. She reached up and touched his lips with hers,

121

then took them away quickly.

He made a face. 'If that's how you kiss Matthew, then poor Matthew! Now,' his arms pulled her closer, 'I'll kiss you like I kiss Margot.'

She struggled. 'Don't do that,' he smiled provocatively, 'Margot never struggles. She's always willing.'

He swooped on her mouth and she was lost. The moments passed and she was sinking down and down and drowning in him again. He pulled her back to the surface at last as a strong swimmer rescues a drowning man. She lay limp in his arms.

When he let her go, she moved away, dazed, and sat down. A key turned in the lock. Beryl and James came in, and Alan met them at the dining-room door. With an effort, Lorraine pulled herself together. She smiled at them as naturally as she could.

'Hallo, you two.' Beryl looked from one to the other. 'Enjoy the concert?'

'Excellent, thanks.'

James asked, 'Matthew here? I thought he might be.'

'No, he took Ann home. Alan brought me back.'

'I suppose,' her mother said, 'that was more sensible. Sit down, Alan. Don't go yet.'

He came back into the room and perched on the arm of Lorraine's chair. He looked down at her, his eyes taunting. 'You don't mind if I share your chair?'

'Would it make any difference if I did?' Her tone was light, but her eyes were sparking.

James was inspecting her. 'You look charming, my dear.'

'She always does,' Alan said, 'even when she's angry, which she often is, with me.'

'Really?' James asked. 'Don't you two get on?'

Alan shook his head. 'We're always quarrelling. She's a real fighter, this one. Fights against everything, even the inevitable.'

Her eyes jerked up to his, full of question, but found no

answer. His eyes were deep and unfathomable and laughing and that irritated her so much she gave him a look intended to chill him to the bone. Instead, he laughed out loud. 'You see, she's fighting me with her eyes now.'

James was such an interested spectator that Lorraine was glad when her mother handed him a hot drink and sat down to sip her own. She said, conversationally, as though Lorraine were not there, 'Don't you think, Alan, she's come out of her shell lately?'

Lorraine was irritated. 'I wish you wouldn't keep turning me into a snail, Mum!'

Alan took her chin and turned her face round. His keen analysing eyes explored hers. 'I don't know about that,' he mused, 'but I think she still has her little hidey-hole she can run to, away from all of us whenever she feels the need —which,' he added with uncomfortable accuracy, 'knowing what I do about Lorraine, is pretty often.'

She jerked her face away and stood up. 'I'm tired.'

Alan rose lazily. 'If that's a hint, I'll take it.'

Beryl and James laughed as he strolled to the door. 'Goodnight, everyone.' He looked at Lorraine, his smile provocative. 'Goodnight, snail.' He raised his hands as if to protect himself and went out.

Christmas was near and Lorraine had bought all her presents. The cake had been made for some time and a thick layer of almond paste covered the top of it. Lorraine decided to ice it one evening when her mother was out. She grew taut when she heard Alan coming downstairs. He stood at the kitchen door watching her smooth the white, semi-liquid icing over the top of the cake.

He commented, 'That looks and smells so delicious, it makes me wish I didn't have to go home for Christmas.'

She looked at him and met his sardonic smile and knew she had imagined a note of wistfulness behind his words.

She replied, in a voice as toneless and disinterested as she

123

could make it, 'You have to go?'

His answer was quiet. 'My mother would be alone if I didn't.'

She placed a miniature pine tree in the centre of the cake and put beside it a Father Christmas figure holding a bulging sack.

'Having visitors for the holiday?' he asked casually.

Lorraine nodded. 'James and Matthew are coming every day.' She lifted the cake carefully across to the side table, then rinsed her hands free of icing sugar. As she dried them she asked, 'Did you want me for something?'

He leaned against a cupboard. 'You remember a promise I made to put together some notes for you about newspapers?'

'I do remember, but I didn't think you meant it.'

He said sarcastically, 'Oh, so I don't keep my word, now? Just another of my many good qualities in your eyes?'

She shrugged and said again, 'I remember.'

'Well, I have made said notes and they're now ready for your use. If you could spare the time, I should like you to come up to my room and we'll go through them together. That is,' his eyes provoked, 'if you can trust an immoral, unscrupulous, lascivious journalist.'

'I—think I can.'

'Quite sure? Because even if you screamed for help it wouldn't be any good. There's no one else in the house to come to your aid.'

She swept past him up the stairs and into his room. He followed her, flung his hand to his head in a dramatic gesture and declaimed, 'By heaven, the girl trusts me!' They laughed together and he closed the door.

He indicated a chair which was drawn up to the table. She sat down and looked with interest at the documents spread out in front of her. She pulled something towards her and began to read it. He removed it. 'That's nothing to do with you.'

'What a pity. It looked so interesting.'

'That's all very well, but we're going to work on your stuff, not mine.'

He drew a pile of notes across the table and thumbed through them. Lorraine watched for a moment, then said, more belligerently than she had intended, 'What I can't understand is how an intelligent, accomplished man like you can bear to lower yourself to the levels required to practise journalism.'

He turned diamond-hard eyes towards her. He said, shaking his head and looking at her as if she were of below-average intelligence, 'Before we go on, it's obvious I shall have to give you a lecture, otherwise all this,' with a sweep of his hand he indicated the notes he had made, 'will be just so much waste paper.' He settled back in his seat, crossed his legs. 'Tell me something. With your obsessive hatred of newspapers and the people who create them, do you consider that all newspaper offices should be forcibly closed and all newspapers banned by law?'

'Of course not.'

'Oh? Why?'

She hesitated, feeling like a dull, hesitant student. 'I suppose—because they're the most important way of letting people know what's going on around them.'

'Right. We agree on something. Let's take it from there. Now, even in a democracy there are things going on behind the scenes which are not brought to light but which should, in the people's own interests, be made public. Agreed?' She nodded. 'You must surely acknowledge that the vital link in this chain of communication is the reporter who's trained to scent out hidden meanings behind events which at first sight seem to be on the level.'

He paused, eyebrows raised, for her response. She nodded again. Satisfied, he went on, 'Now if this reporter can reveal something which is being suppressed by the powers-that-be and which ordinary people have a right to know, then the reporter, in his privileged position, is doing an invaluable public service. You're with me?'

'All the way.'

'Good. Now having got that settled, tell me, is every individual educated to our standards?'

'Of course not.'

'Then, since a newspaper's most important function is to communicate, journalists must write so that the large majority of people can understand what they're saying.'

She nodded.

'We can't indulge,' he went on with a smile, 'in the long words you so love teaching your defenceless pupils. No one would buy newspapers if we did, simply because they wouldn't understand them. Therefore, as you in your prim and proper way would put it, we have to reduce good quality English to words of one syllable so that nine out of ten people will understand what we're talking about.'

Grudgingly Lorraine had to agree that he was right. He looked at her for a few moments, then held out his hand.

'Pax?' he asked quietly.

She put her hand in his, and said innocently, 'Surely you mean "peace"?'

His fingers tightened. '*Touché*. As you say,' he smiled mockingly, 'in the words of the masses—peace.'

They worked on, side by side, until Alan said, 'I feel in need of some refreshment. Any chance of some coffee?'

Lorraine got up immediately and Alan followed her down to the kitchen. 'I'll help,' he offered, but instead of helping, he sat astride the kitchen stool and talked. He carried the tray upstairs and they drank the coffee and worked again.

'This is nice,' he said suddenly.

'What is?'

'Being at peace with you.' He stretched out his legs and clasped his hands behind his head. 'War between nations is

126

futile, but war between individuals is even worse.' He smiled out of the corner of his eye. 'Especially when the combatant is female, excessively belligerent and so—er—attractive.'

Lorraine stiffened at once and he patted her hand. 'Calm down, hedgehog.'

The phone rang and they both rose together. 'Stay there,' he said. 'I'll call if it's for you.'

He went down and Lorraine heard him say, 'Margot? What do you want? I can't understand you. Have you been drinking? You've just come from a party? Me? I'm working. Who am I working on? Miss Ferrers, if you must know, and the word's not "on", it's "with". Yes, I know she's only a schoolteacher and no, you never get anywhere with them.' He laughed. 'But there's no harm in trying, is there?'

Lorraine began to collect her papers. Alan was saying, 'You don't mean to say you're jealous—of Miss Ferrers?' His tone was incredulous, then he listened again. His voice hardened. 'No, as you say, she's not my type. Yes, you can come round if you like.' He slammed the receiver down and strode up the stairs. He caught Lorraine at the door and pushed her back into the room. 'Where are you going? We haven't finished our work yet.'

'As far as I'm concerned, we have. I'll now make way for your lady visitor.'

'You're staying.'

'I'm not.' She tried to push past him and got her hand to the door handle. He turned the key. 'I repeat, you're staying. I have my reasons.'

He gripped her arm and pushed her into a chair, then went on talking as though nothing had happened. 'Now, where were we? Ah, yes.' He began speaking, but Lorraine did not take in a word of it.

She said, between her teeth, 'Will you let me out?'

'No,' he answered mildly, taking his pen and adding

127

something to the notes, 'not even if you start assaulting me as you did once before.'

The doorbell rang. 'That was quick,' he commented. 'She must have got a lift. Trust Margot!'

As he went to the door, Lorraine followed. He pushed her back and locked her in. She rattled the door handle, and he laughed as he went down the stairs.

Lorraine knew she had to compose herself to meet Margot, and she needed the help of all the poise she possessed, inadequate though it was, to meet the girl's fuddled but hostile stare.

Alan's smile was wicked as he watched them. Margot turned to him. 'Darling, I thought you'd be alone by now.'

He grinned maliciously. 'I can hardly turn a woman out if she doesn't want to leave me, can I?'

Lorraine choked back her anger and turned pale with the effort. Alan watched her and went towards her. She stood up, but he sat on the side of her chair, put his arm round her and pulled her down. She tried to move away, but his fingers dug viciously into her flesh.

'Darling,' Margot said plaintively, 'what are you up to? Playing off one woman against the other?'

'Yes. I'm trying to make you both jealous.'

'Darling, you won't make me jealous. I know you're mine.' She took his hand and pulled him to another chair. She pushed him down and sat on his knee, put her arms round his neck and kissed him. 'Now you kiss me,' she said. He kissed her cheek. 'No, here.' She touched her lips with a finger and he kissed her mouth, then put her off his knee.

'You need sobering up, sweetie.'

She shook her head slowly. 'I like being this way. It makes me forget my inhibitions.'

He laughed cynically. 'You—inhibited?' He said to Lorraine, 'Any strong coffee going?'

Lorraine gathered up her things for the second time.

'You heard what Miss French said. She likes being that way.'

She went out of the door and he followed. He said, narrowly, 'Don't be so bitchy.'

She turned on him. 'What else do you expect me to be? You keep me in there solely to make your girl-friend jealous and to demonstrate to me how clever you are in handling the opposite sex, and then you expect me to get you out of a tight spot!' She lost her temper and her caution. Her voice rose harshly as she tried to stem the tears. 'Why don't you go back in there and give her what she's so brazenly asking for? Or isn't it within your masculine powers to gratify her wishes?' His fingers curled into his palms and his eyes roared into life, but she persisted with even greater bitterness, 'She's obviously more compliant and more—more willing in that condition, so why try to sober her up? She's easy game. I'm not. You'd have to work a darned sight harder to catch me, wouldn't you? So why bother?'

Her eyes grew blurred as the tears took over and she heard him say in a voice deliberate and grating, 'For that, my little *flower*,' he rolled the word round his tongue, 'I'll do just as you advise.' He slammed the door in her face.

She sat on her bed and covered her face with her hands. The tears trickled through her fingers and down the backs of her hands. She started sobbing uncontrollably and threw herself down sideways on to her pillow. She was as she had always been—a girl alone. She knew she had nothing for any man. Against a woman like Margot, who could ever hope to win?

She was still crying when Margot left some time later. She dragged herself up and got ready for bed. She put on her housecoat and opened her door to go across to the bathroom.

At that moment Alan's door opened. He too seemed to be intending to wash. His tie had been removed, his shirt was unbuttoned to the waist. When Lorraine looked at him, he stood still. His gaze roamed over her face, patchy and red with crying, and he stared into her eyes which were swollen and desolate. He made an abrupt movement forward, but she ran across the landing and closed the bathroom door. She heard him go back into his room and wait for her to finish washing.

The following evening, Alan took his dishes into the kitchen and handed them to Beryl who was standing at the sink. Lorraine was drying up and she was dressed to go out with Matthew.

Alan ignored her and spoke a few words to Beryl. As he turned to go, Lorraine said awkwardly, 'I'm afraid I forgot to say thank you last night for your help.' She concentrated on the cup she was drying. 'I really am grateful for all those notes and your advice.'

She looked at him and his face told her nothing. He nodded. She forced herself to go on. 'I'm going to try them out on the girls and see how they react to them.'

He nodded again, his face serious, almost cold. The doorbell rang and she flung down the tea towel and ran past him to open the door. Matthew's arms were outstretched as he stepped inside and she escaped into the welcome and the comfort of them. He kissed her on the cheek and then on the lips and she heard Alan stride up the stairs and close his door.

Matthew took Lorraine to the small theatre in the town to watch a local amateur group perform a Shaw play. The actors were surprisingly good and the audience applauded enthusiastically. Afterwards he took her for a meal at a restaurant nearby.

He asked her, keeping his eyes on the tablecloth, 'Are your affections still engaged in the same quarter? In other words, is it still Alan?'

She nodded. 'I'm sorry, Matthew.'

He laughed a little ruefully. 'I expected it. It stands out a mile. You only come alive when he's near you.'

This alarmed her. 'Does it show that much?'

'Only because I know. All the same, I don't give up hope.'

He took her home and they kissed goodnight in the car. 'I like you so much,' Lorraine whispered. 'If only——'

'I know what you're going to say. Don't.'

Lorraine got out and he raised his hand and drove away.

CHAPTER VIII

IT was the last week of term and no one was in the mood for routine work. The class tests were over and the girls wanted to relax and get into the spirit of Christmas. Lorraine decided that a change of subject was as good a way as any to humour them, so on Monday morning she went to school with her briefcase packed to capacity with newspapers. They ranged from the 'quality' journals to the most popular dailies.

From the first-formers upwards the girls responded with enthusiasm to the exercise. They spread the newspapers over the floor—there was no other flat surface large enough to take them all—and they studied design and style and tried to determine the type of readership each newspaper aimed at.

They noted the different treatment of the same story in each paper, compared the construction and length of sentences. They counted the syllables of the words used in the 'quality' papers and compared them with the simpler words used in the others.

They cut out reports of incidents and pasted them on to large sheets of cardboard and pinned them to the wall. With the help of Alan's notes, Lorraine led them in a discussion of the power newspaper proprietors had in forming public opinion, the politics of each newspaper and the trick which some of the less worthy papers used of putting forward opinion as fact.

Next term, she told them, they would be asked to do a project on the newspaper industry and suggested that, in the meantime, they should study as many different papers as their pocket money would allow them to buy.

At break, while Lorraine told Ann what she was doing,

other teachers gathered round to listen. One or two looked distinctly disapproving and it became clear to Lorraine that the subject she was tackling was a complete innovation. They hinted that no one had dared to do such a thing before. Was Miss Ferrers sure, one of them asked, that the headmistress would approve?

'You can hardly claim that it's in the syllabus,' complained Miss Grimson, one of the older teachers in the English department and a friend of the headmistress. 'Neither will it help the girls through their examinations and that, in my opinion, is the prime aim of the tuition they receive here.'

'It may not be in the syllabus,' Lorraine answered and surprised herself with her new-found revolutionary fervour, 'but it certainly makes them think for themselves and appreciate what is going on outside the solid brick walls of this rather ageing school.'

This statement effectively reduced her audience to two or three, and she and Ann were soon left alone.

'My word,' Ann said, 'you've got a bit more spirit these days, Lorraine. Could it be your journalist friend's influence?'

She admitted reluctantly, 'Alan certainly has helped to change my ideas,' and she added bitterly, 'when he can spare the time from the fabulous Margot.'

Ann looked sorry for her. 'You're up against formidable competition there, dear. She's got looks, clothes-sense, man-appeal—everything, in fact, except intelligence, and when you've got all the others—my dear, does that matter?'

Lorraine told her what had happened when she and Alan were working together and Margot had called.

Ann frowned. 'Why did he want to keep you there?'

'To make her jealous. Why else?'

'But he'd hardly need to do that. Even when she shows interest in other men, she never really lets Alan go. He's always there for her to run back to, as he admitted himself.'

She sighed. 'All the same, it's interesting. But take another word of advice from Auntie. Get him out of your system. Concentrate on Matthew. If you don't know it already, he's yours for the asking, and a nicer man you could hardly wish for.'

Term ended a week before Christmas. One afternoon, Lorraine was standing at the bus stop loaded with shopping when Alan's car drew up beside her. He opened the front passenger door. 'Get in, Lorraine.'

Thankfully she sidled into the car, arms still clutching her shopping, and he drove into the traffic. I was almost dark and the shop windows were bright with lights and festive decorations.

'Looking forward to Christmas?' he asked, without taking his eyes from the road.

'Reasonably so. Are you?'

'Reasonably so.' He echoed her words and they laughed. 'I go tomorrow, you know.'

She knew only too well. It was a fact that wouldn't leave her alone. 'All those hours,' she was thinking, 'when I'll have to look as though I'm enjoying myself, when all the time I'll be longing for the sound of his voice and the sight of his face.'

'Would you take pity on a lonely journalist, Lorraine, and come out to dinner with me?'

She was so shaken by his invitation and the abrupt way he issued it that it took her a few minutes to respond.

'If you're otherwise engaged,' his voice was off-hand, 'just say so. There's no need to spare my feelings. According to you, I have precious few to spare.'

She answered, still hesitant from surprise, 'Well, I've got nothing much to do, so yes, thank you. Matthew's not coming this evening——'

'And Margot's gone to report a dress show,' he countered at once.

They laughed. 'Two people without their chosen part-ners.' He flicked her a provocative look. 'So we accept each other as second best. That's right, isn't it?'

She nodded and turned her face resolutely to the win-dow, watching the passers-by trundling shopping bags on wheels, pushing prams and standing, arms full of parcels, waiting patiently, as she had been doing, in the long bus queues.

'Will your mother mind?'

'No. James is coming to a meal, so they'll probably prefer to be alone. Afterwards they're going to friends for the evening.'

'Right. Seven-thirty,' he said as he drove into the garage. He grinned. 'I'll call for you.'

She smiled back. 'I can't wait for your ring at the doorbell.'

'It's more likely to be a hammering at your bedroom door, especially if you're so much as a minute late. If you are, I'll walk in and kidnap you.'

Lorraine did not even try to contain her happiness. When she spoke to her mother, it was there in her eyes. Beryl looked at her curiously and asked, with a tinge of anxiety, 'Does Matthew know?'

'Matthew?' Lorraine was puzzled. 'No. In any case, he wouldn't mind. He's not coming this evening.'

'I just wondered, dear. It's only that his father and I . . .'

Lorraine ran from the kitchen. She could not bear to hear what her mother was trying to tell her. 'Lorraine and Matthew, Matthew and Lorraine . . .' They were so plainly coupled together in her mother's and future stepfather's minds that she felt as though the doors of a strong-room were closing on her cutting off all possible hope of escape.

She put on the dress she had worn for the dance. It was thin, but it was right for a dinner date and it was one she thought Alan admired. She met him on the landing and he looked at his watch.

'Five minutes early. An exceptional as well as a beautiful woman.'

'I never listen to flattery,' she tossed over her shoulder as she ran downstairs in front of him to get her coat.

'That's the trouble,' he murmured, following her.

'You look smart, too,' she told him, admiringly.

'I never listen to flattery,' he mimicked, and she laughed.

'I don't know why you're so happy,' he said, with a gleam in his eye. 'It's only me you're going out with, not Matthew.'

'And I make a poor substitute for Margot,' she reminded him.

'There is no substitute for Margot,' he stated solemnly as though he were repeating an advertising slogan. But Lorraine felt that she had been put in her place and it turned down the heat of her happiness a few degrees.

'Where are we going?' she asked as they left the town and drove along winding country lanes.

'To a place called the Pine Needles. They do a good meal. I've been there before on a press ticket to dinners and official functions. It's newly built. None of your olde Tudor beams and low ceilings.'

It was, in fact, of oddly modern design. To Lorraine, her vision bedazzled by the intensity of her happiness, it had the look of a gnome's house in a child's story book, with its pointed gables supporting deeply sloping roofs, and its multitude of tiny windows bright with coloured lamps.

In the dining-room the lights were low and the atmosphere intimate. They sat side by side, on a bench seat in an alcove. The menu, standing on the table, was large and impressive and read like a book. Lorraine noted the prices and said, uncertainly, 'It's a bit expensive, Alan.'

'I'm paying, Lorraine, so go ahead and choose the dearest items if you want. It's not often my second-best girl-friend comes out with her second-best boy-friend. In fact,' he smiled down at her and in the half-light his face seemed

136

very near, 'she might never have another chance to do so, so she'd better make the most of it.'

'Why?' she asked, her heart lying somewhere at her feet. 'Are you opting out of bachelorhood and getting married?'

He inspected the menu with the concentrated interest of a detective searching for fingerprints. 'Could be.'

'So,' she said, driven on by her misery, 'Margot's achieved the impossible. She's tamed you and fixed the lead to your collar and she's in the process of housetraining you for domesticity. In fact,' she added bitterly and without caring how much she gave away, 'you're now the finished product—the potential husband.'

Now he was smiling hugely at the menu, as though it were a great joke. 'You're so right,' he murmured. 'And my potential will be realised as soon as possible after the ring has been pushed on to the girl's wedding finger.'

She snorted and flung down her copy of the menu.

'You said it,' he reminded her, still grinning. 'You put the words into my mouth and being a journalist, how could I resist following you up?'

The waiter appeared from nowhere and hovered obsequiously in the dimness. While Alan ordered, Lorraine observed the other diners, noting their comparative intimacy with a powerful stab of envy, and concluding that she and Alan were sitting farther apart than any of the other couples dining there.

Alan broke into her thoughts. 'Now, having taken a survey of your immediate surroundings in a fashion which would do credit to an experienced journalist, tell me, Miss Ferrers, what are your conclusions?'

She shook her head, glad that the shadows were there to hide the colour in her cheeks. But he saw her confusion and persisted, 'Now you've really got me interested. Tell me what you're thinking.'

Reluctantly she answered, 'Only that the rather—seduc-

137

tive atmosphere has had its effect and . . .' Her voice trailed off.

'And?' His eyes flicked over the other couples and he leaned back and smiled broadly. 'I see what you mean. Well, that's easy to remedy.' He moved so close to her that their arms were pressed together, but Lorraine edged away.

He looked hurt. 'Why did you do that?'

'How can we eat properly if our arms haven't room to move up and down to feed our mouths?'

He laughed with something like relief. 'Is that all? We'll get together at the coffee stage if you're so inclined.' He looked askance at her, as if testing her reaction. 'I'm always willing to get as close as possible to an attractive woman.'

She drew herself in, trying to ward off the pain his words were inflicting. She felt that everything he was saying was intended to put her back in her place, to make her realise that, to him, she was just another girl whom he had invited to dine with him.

They talked through the meal and finished with coffee. Lorraine had the cup to her mouth when she felt Alan's hand smoothing her long hair. She lowered the empty cup to the saucer and his arm crept round her waist. She tensed, but he moved no nearer, so she relaxed.

She heard him whisper her name and her head turned swiftly towards him. 'Lorraine——' he said again, then realised they were not alone. A man stood in front of them, a tall man Lorraine remembered vaguely.

'So it's like that, is it, Alan?' he joked, and Alan took away his arm. His whole bearing changed, his manner hardened and his eyes became like granite.

'Hallo, Jim. What are you doing here? I didn't know you visited such expensive places.'

'I don't usually, Alan, but there's a nice little thing I've met I wanted to impress.' He looked at Lorraine. 'Surely we've had the pleasure of meeting somewhere?'

'You have. At my desk one afternoon. The lady came to

borrow my key.'

'Ah yes,' Jim clicked his fingers. 'You're not—you can't be that shy little schoolteacher?'

'Right first time,' said Alan, showing irritation.

Jim whistled and said, 'Damn. If only I had my camera with me! Wait till I tell the boys!'

Alan's lips contracted into a thin line. He said bitingly, 'Will you leave us alone and get back to your own little piece?'

'Implying you want to be left to enjoy your little piece? All right, friend, I can take a hint.'

He sloped off. Alan's mood had changed beyond repair. His eyes were cold as they looked at Lorraine and she wondered what she had done to merit his annoyance.

'Finished?' he asked abruptly. 'Right, we'll go.'

He paid the bill and swept out in front of her to the car park.

'What's the matter?' she asked as they settled in the car. 'Afraid he'll tell Margot?'

'If it pleases you to think that, yes,' he snapped back.

Lorraine subsided and did battle with her tears. She did not want to let anything spoil the wonderful evening. 'Where are we going?' she muttered. 'Home?'

'We're going for a walk,' he said shortly. 'Been to your hill lately?'

'No. Wrong time of year.'

'Well, we're going there now.'

She sat up. 'What, in the dark? In December?'

'I told you, I want to walk.' He glanced at her briefly. 'If you're not game, I'll drop you home and go alone.'

'Of course I'm game.'

He swung the car off the road and they started walking. With no torch and no moonlight to help them, they had to feel the way through the bracken and undergrowth. He took her hand and they started climbing to the summit. The twigs crackled as they trod steadily upwards and the strangeness of the situation was overlaid by a primitive sense of awe at the sight of the massive silent shapes hemming them in in the bitter stillness.

The chill wind made Lorraine clutch at her coat collar. She shivered, wishing she had worn a cardigan over her thin dress. Although her winter coat was warm, it was not sufficient to keep out the biting cold. The sky was clear, showing the stars and threatening frost later.

Alan's arm lifted to her waist and pulled her to him as if to shelter her. They were like one person striding up the hill. Here was the quiet man again, she thought, the man beneath the tough exterior, the man she loved so much.

'Anyone would think,' she laughed, 'that we were in love.'

'And they would be right. We are, aren't we?'

Her head turned sharply. 'You mean—you mean with other people?'

He laughed now. 'Why the surprise? What else did you think I meant?'

She was silent, and could have kicked herself for her false hope and her naïveté.

After a while he said, 'You're very quiet.'

'So are you.'

'I like it that way.'

'So do I.'

He tightened his hold on her waist. 'Now there's an unusual woman. She likes silence. So different from Margot.'

'No doubt,' she took him up savagely, 'you have your own special way of keeping Margot quiet.'

'I certainly have,' he countered. 'How clever of you to know that.' He added as an afterthought, 'Anyway, I could never do this with Margot.'

'Why worry?' she threw back at him with desperate sarcasm, 'when there are so many—other things you can do with Margot.'

'You're so right,' he agreed, his voice deep with amusement.

She jerked away, but he pulled at her arm and forced her to stand still and face him. She could make out the outline of his mouth and she thought it was uplifted in a smile. Angry that he still would not take her seriously, she tried to free herself, but his hands clamped on to her shoulders. She knew he was playing with her and she wanted to cry out to him to stop.

He held her firmly at arm's length until she was still, then he drew her against him and his mouth covered hers. The kiss had come and gone in the space of a few seconds, but she doubted if her legs had the strength to keep her upright.

'Pax?' he whispered.

'Peace,' she whispered back, and they climbed the hill again.

'We've made it,' he said, as they reached the summit, and stood looking down at the blackness below, pierced by moving lights and street lamps stringing out into the far distance.

'In the daytime,' Lorraine murmured, 'this is a view I love. I've escaped to this hill so many times. Either I leave my problems behind me or I bring them up here to work out a solution. It never fails.'

She glanced up at him shyly and realised how much of herself she had given away. He seemed to sense the reason for her sudden reticence.

'It's all right, I know you have problems. You'll probably always have them. You're that sort of person. You get rid of one and find another.' They laughed together.

He took her arm and entwined his fingers with hers. 'So you've never been up here in the dark before? Then this is a "first" for both of us.' His fingers tightened. 'Something to remember each other by when our ways have finally parted, when you're busy being faithful to your husband, whoever he may be, and I, as you so picturesquely put it earlier this evening, am being led about on a long lead by the woman I eventually marry.'

She knew he was smiling by the sound of his voice. The street lights far below curled and blurred into melting yellows and golds. She could not trust herself to speak.

'Come on,' he said, 'you're supposed to laugh.' When she failed to respond he asked, 'What's the matter?' Gently he took her chin and turned her head to face him. Even in the darkness she knew he must have seen the tears, but he made no comment.

She shivered. 'You're cold,' he said. 'We must go.' They started down the hill and he took her hand and soon they were running the rest of the way. In the car, Alan draped the rug round her shoulders, but still she shivered.

At home, he pushed her into an armchair and made a hot drink.

'Soon be Christmas Eve,' he remarked, sitting down opposite her. 'Getting excited?'

'Getting excited when you won't be here?' she thought, and shook her head. 'I used to as a child, but not any more.'

'But Matthew will be coming for Christmas.'

She pretended to brighten. 'So he will. Matthew's fun, and so is his father.'

'A nice little family party.'

She looked at him and wondered if she had imagined the sour note in his voice. But of course, she remembered, he would be leaving Margot behind and that would depress him.

'Never mind,' she tried to soothe him, 'you'll be able to see Margot as soon as you get back.'

Now it was his turn to brighten. 'So I will.'

Lorraine began to shiver again and Alan looked concerned. 'I think you'd better go to bed. Surely it's not necessary to wait up for your mother?'

'I do feel tired. Perhaps I will go up.'

He put his arm round her shoulders. 'Come along. I must see my second-best girl-friend right to her door.'

They stood on the landing. 'Goodnight, Alan,' Lorraine said, and started to move away.

'Just a minute.' His hand caught hers. 'I'll be leaving early in the morning. Before you're awake, probably.' He pulled her towards him and she was too tired to resist. His gaze wandered over her face and stopped at her mouth. 'Your lips ask to be kissed. They're inviting me right now.'

She leaned away from him, resenting the way he always made her feel as though she were egging him on and that he, not too unwillingly—she was after all a woman—complied.

'Just like Margot's do?' she taunted back.

He shook his head and smiled. 'No. Margot's much more brazen in her invitation.'

'Meaning, I suppose, that I want the same thing, but my tactics are more subtle?'

'Definitely. Of course you want the same thing. All women do.'

'Even dull respectable ones like me?'

'Yes, even dull respectable ones like you want to tie a man to them for the rest of his life.' She struggled to free herself angrily, but he tightened his hold. 'You can't deny it. You told me so yourself.'

She struggled again. 'That's not true. You've twisted my words. But of course,' she sneered, 'I forgot your profession. You twist words by trade. All journalists do.' She thought he would be angry, but he laughed, and this annoyed her more than his anger. 'What I said was,' she went on, 'that *I* would stick to a man for life—*my* life. If he didn't want me and threw me overboard—well, that would just be my bad luck, wouldn't it?'

His smile was cynical as he said, 'Anyway, whether a woman is brazen or subtle in her invitation makes no difference. Either way flatters my ego no end.'

He was laughing at her again and his refusal to take her seriously made her desperate in her attempts to free herself. He lowered his head, seeking her mouth, but she twisted away and broke free of him with a violent jerk.

'Why can't you leave me alone?' she cried. 'I'm not Margot. Or are you so desperate for a substitute that even *I* will do?'

They stood apart, breathing heavily. His eyes flared for a terrifying moment like tinder soaked in petrol, but his anger was shortlived and cynicism took over. He narrowed his eyes and lounged against the wall, arms folded.

'Whoever would have thought,' he said, 'that our shy little schoolteacher possessed such a vitriolic tongue? You'd better watch out, my *sweet* Miss Ferrers. One day your acidity might boomerang and hurt you more than the person you're throwing it at.'

The front door opened and closed and Beryl looked up the stairs. 'Hallo, you two,' she called. 'Saying goodnight?' Lorrraine was glad that her mother didn't seem to expect an answer. 'You'll be off early tomorrow, Alan? It's a good way to Manchester from here, isn't it?'

He went down the stairs to talk to her and Lorraine ran into her bedroom. Slowly she grew calmer and her thoughts arranged themselves into a more coherent, logical order. It was then that she realised she had not thanked Alan for taking her out. She listened until she heard him coming up the stairs. She stood up resolutely and leaving her pride behind her, went on to the landing.

'Alan?' He stopped in his doorway, turned an unsmiling face towards her. 'Thank you, Alan, for taking me out to dinner.' Her voice sounded annoyingly submissive, but his lack of response unnerved her.

He looked her indolently up and down, then without a word, shut the door on her. When she awoke in the morning, he had gone.

CHAPTER IX

It was Christmas Eve. Lorraine went past Alan's room on her way downstairs and there was an emptiness inside her that she could hardly bear. He had been gone for only a few hours, but already it seemed like a month.

'You look pale, dear.' Her mother's eyes, reminiscent of childhood, stared anxiously at her face. 'Sure you feel all right?'

Lorraine was not sure, but she said, 'Yes, I'm all right.' She did not tell her mother that her legs felt weak and she had a curiously lethargic feeling about her. She had convinced herself that it was due to Alan's absence and the longing inside her that would not be stilled.

'We've got the mince-pies to make,' Beryl was saying, 'and the parcels to finish wrapping. You know, dear, you should have got something for Alan. I kept telling you, you've got a present for everyone else. He'll be upset, I'm sure he will.'

'Why should I bother to get him anything?' Lorraine asked defiantly, trying to quieten the stirring of her conscience. 'He's not one of the family and he won't be here. Anyway,' she said, doing her best to convince herself that she was right and her mother wrong, 'when could I have given it to him?'

'Before he left.'

'But that would have embarrassed him, because he wouldn't have got me anything.' She shook her head. 'No, it's best as it is, with neither of us giving each other a present.'

'Listen, dear, I didn't want to tell you, but Alan left something in his room and it's got a funny message on it. I think it must be for you. It said something about a flower.'

Lorraine laughed, then experienced a curious desire to cry. So he had not forgotten her after all. 'Oh dear, you could be right, Mum. I'd better slip out and buy him something before the shops close.'

After lunch she searched the menswear section of the large department store, deciding in the end to buy a tie. She took a long time over the selection of it. The one she chose was tasteful but bright and she felt it would please him. It was expensive, but she willingly gave the money to the assistant.

She took it home and wrapped it and started counting the hours to the time when she would be able to put it into his hands.

She worked with her mother for the rest of the day, preparing the house for the visitors. They would not be staying overnight, but would arrive each day immediately after breakfast. As the day passed, Lorraine felt progressively worse, but she kept it from her mother until the early evening. All the work had been done. The turkey was stuffed and ready to cook, the mince-pies were put away in tins and the presents were piled under the small Christmas tree which Beryl had carried home from the local market.

'It's no good,' Lorraine sighed, sinking into a chair. 'I'll have to give in and go to bed.'

Her mother looked worried. 'I thought you hadn't been up to the mark all day, dear. You look quite ill. Go up now, Lorrie, and you'll probably feel better in the morning.'

'I'll have to, won't I? I can't leave you to cope alone tomorrow.'

As she went up to bed, she looked at Alan's closed door. Surely, she thought, it couldn't be his absence that was having such a disastrous effect on her?

She drank the hot milk and took the tablets which her mother gave her. 'You'll feel better tomorrow,' she said, soothing her as though she were a little girl again.

But next morning Lorraine felt worse. She could not find

146

the energy to put a foot out of bed. Despite the difficult circumstances, her mother took it well.

'It must be the flu, dear. You'll have to stay where you are.'

'But how will you manage alone?' Lorraine protested feebly.

Her mother did manage, but not alone. James rolled up his sleeves, put on an apron and helped her all day.

'Your father's wonderful,' Lorraine said to Matthew as he sat on the bed holding her hand.

'So's his son,' he said, grinning.

'He'll make my mother a wonderful husband,' Lorraine remarked, ignoring his words.

'His son's on the marriage market and going for a song,' he persisted, still grinning. 'Any offers?'

Lorraine laughed, but found it an effort. Matthew mused, as if to himself, 'In her weak state, if I'm persistent enough, she might give in.'

She turned her head to the wall and he took the hint. 'See you later, love.' He crept out.

Lorraine could not eat the Christmas dinner that her mother carried up to her. She slept most of the day and in the evening they all gathered in her bedroom, their arms full of presents which they had, with great strength of mind, delayed opening until she felt like joining in.

Matthew opened Lorraine's alternately with his own. James had bought her a sweater to match the skirt which her mother had given her. Matthew's gift was a double row of pearls.

'Your mother,' he said with a twinkle, 'got so tired of lending you hers, she persuaded me to give you some.'

'It's not true,' her mother laughed. 'He bought them of his own free will.'

Matthew put the gloves she had given him to his heart.

'Er—Lorrie,' her mother had gone out of the room and returned with one more present in her hand. It was the one

Lorraine had been waiting for. 'This is what I found in Alan's room. It says, "To the flower that refuses to grow in my garden, From the Florist." Could it be for you? If it is, I wish I knew what he was talking about.'

Matthew was laughing, James was puzzled but amused and Beryl was a little irritated because she couldn't understand what it meant.

Without going into too many details, Lorraine explained what the greeting referred to. She removed the wrapping paper and discovered that it was a record in an attractive cover. It was the New World Symphony and Lorraine did not even try to hide her tears.

Matthew knew the reason for them, but her mother said, 'Never mind, you can give him your present when he comes back, dear.'

'There's one thing he's forgotten,' Lorraine said, 'I haven't got a record player.'

'Oh, he probably intends to give you that next Christmas,' Matthew put in, and everyone laughed.

Christmas Day was almost at an end. Lorraine was too depressed to read the magazines on her bedside table. She turned her back on them and was drifting into a light sleep when the telephone rang. It startled her into awareness and a tingling sensation ran through her when she heard her mother say,

'Hallo, Alan. Had a nice Christmas? Yes, thank you. Very quiet, especially with Lorraine in bed. Yes, she's not at all well. We think it was the flu. Alan, she loved your present. What, you loved hers? Oh dear, she's going to give you one, Alan, she really is. You're going to collect it in person?' Beryl laughed. 'Yes, I'll tell her that. And I'll tell her that, too. It might cheer her up. Is your mother there? Why, hallo, Nancy. How are you?' And so the conversation went on.

Because Alan had gone, Lorraine stopped listening. The fact that he had phoned at all had an electrifying effect on

148

her. The blood began to race through her veins, her pulse rate quickened alarmingly and everything around her—the presents, the decorations Matthew had brought in to cheer her up—assumed a meaning and a promise beyond belief.

Her mother came upstairs. 'That was Nancy and Alan. They're coming here tomorrow evening.'

Lorraine's eyes opened wider. 'But Alan's not due back until——'

'I know, but he's returning early for some reason. And his mother is coming with him. She'll be staying for a few days. She can have Alan's room and he can sleep in the lounge on the chair-bed. He was very sorry to hear about you and hoped you didn't catch a chill the other night when he took you out. He said you went for a walk and it was cold.'

Lorraine nodded, but didn't elaborate. 'What else did he say?'

She paused at the door. 'Only that he sent his love.'

That night, Lorraine slept well. She was looking so much brighter next day that Matthew remarked on it.

'I'm beginning to think you're a fraud,' he said. 'I think your illness was psychological and that the "cure" was on the phone last night.'

By the time Alan and his mother arrived, Lorraine was sitting up in bed wearing her mother's pink bed-jacket.

'You still look washed out, Lorrie,' Beryl said, just before they got there. 'It's years since Nancy's seen you. It's a pity you won't look as pretty as you usually do.'

When they walked in, Lorraine's heart was throbbing like a beating of drums. Nancy Darby came first. She was of medium height, although beside her son, she seemed short. Her hair was grey, her form slight and compared with Beryl, she looked her age. Her eyes were keen, like Alan's, but her smile was genuine and warm, without a trace of the cynicism which so often marred her son's.

She embraced Lorraine. 'My word,' she looked into her

149

face, 'how you've grown up! It's—let me see—a good ten years since I saw her, isn't it, Beryl? You and Henry brought her up to us one weekend. You stayed a couple of nights.'

'Where was Alan?' Lorraine asked, without looking at him.

'Oh, away somewhere as usual. Before he came to live here, you hadn't seen him since you were a baby.'

'So we've met before, have we?' Alan's voice came over his mother's shoulder.

'If you can call it meeting,' his mother laughed. 'If I remember correctly,' she looked at Beryl, 'Lorraine was two years old and Alan was twelve.'

'That's right,' Beryl agreed. 'She kept pestering him because she wanted to sit on his knee and he wouldn't let her.'

Alan threw back his head and laughed and his laughter grew louder as his mother went on, 'We watched her pulling at his legs and trying to clamber up on him while he was reading a book. She kept on so long that in the end he put his book down, gave her a good spanking and sat her down hard. Then he went on with his reading.'

'And Lorraine screamed her head off and I had to pacify her,' Beryl added. 'I remember it so clearly.'

'I wish I did,' said Alan, rubbing his hands. 'I obviously knew how to treat women even in those early days.'

His mother turned her head and asked, 'What would you do to her now, son, if she tried to sit on your knee?'

'My word,' his eyes glinted at the prospect, 'there's no knowing what I'd do to her. No knowing at all.'

Lorraine turned pink at the look in his eyes and changed the subject. 'Why did you come back early, Alan?'

His mother answered for him. 'He said he could have left it until tomorrow, but he wanted to see a girl. He wouldn't tell me which girl. I can't keep up with my son's amorous adventures.'

'Oh,' said Beryl, 'he means that Margot, don't you, Alan?' There was no response from Alan. 'She's always ringing him and coming here. My dear,' she rested her hand on Nancy's arm, 'you should see her. Very glam.' She turned to Alan. 'Is it the real thing at last, Alan? Or shouldn't I ask that?'

'It depends what you mean,' he said, with a narrow, calculating expression, 'by the "real thing".' He smiled at Lorraine. 'Now as an experienced teacher of English, Miss Ferrers, how would you define "real" and "thing"?'

Lorraine turned her head from the malice in his eyes. Beryl nudged Nancy. 'He's not going to tell you, dear. He's really saying "Mind your own business", aren't you, Alan?'

'Yes,' he said, politely but firmly. Soon after that they all went out, but Alan came back on his own.

'Hallo,' he said, as if seeing her for the first time.

'Thank you for my lovely present, Alan,' she said, stretching out her hand. He took it. 'The only trouble is—no record player.'

He laughed. 'That was the whole point. I gave you a record to inveigle you up to my room to play it on mine. Once I get you there—well, you never know what might happen. I might even spank you, like I did when you were two.' They laughed together and he sat on the bed.

'Keep away,' she warned. 'You might catch what I've had.'

He frowned. 'I'm so sorry, Lorraine. You probably caught a chill the other night. You kept saying you were cold. It must have spoilt your Christmas.' He looked at her and anticipation gleamed in his eyes. 'I've come to collect my present.'

Hastily, trying to ward off what she thought he had in mind, she tugged a packet from under her pillow. 'It's here, Alan.'

He shook his head, 'I don't mean what you mean. This is my present.' He bent low, but she turned her head.

'No, this is your present.' She pushed it into his hands and watched him unwrap it. 'Not very original,' she apologised, 'but——' She stopped, unable to believe that the appreciation in his eyes was genuine.

He held it up against his shirt. 'I shall wear it until it becomes threadbare,' he said, 'which, judging by what it must have cost, will probably take years. Now *I'm* going to say "thank you".'

He put his mouth to hers and kept it there a long time, and she had no wish to resist. 'Missed me?' he whispered.

She nodded and knew it was an admission which gave him entry to her heart.

The quick response in his eyes told her that he knew it too. 'What?' he asked, almost gloating, 'with Matthew here?'

Lorraine had nothing to say. His arms slipped round her and his kiss was warm and gentle. When he had finished, he gazed at the love in her eyes. 'I've won, haven't I? I've won the battle.'

She felt a sickening pain inside her. 'What battle?'

He whispered, 'I've got you where I said I'd never allow you to go. You can't deny it. You're a flower in my garden now.' His smile tugged at her heart like a puppeteer manipulating the strings. With his next words he let the strings go slack and her heart flopped, lifeless and discarded.

His voice sharpened as he spoke through his teeth and acted the villain, 'You know what I do with the flowers in my garden, don't you? I cut them down when they're in full bloom, thus,' he ran a finger across her throat from one side to the other, 'and I throw them away, like the weeds they are.' He put aside his villainy and relaxed. 'So now you know what's coming to you.'

He smiled and there was something else besides victory in his smile, something elusive and tantalising that Lorraine could not interpret. 'And there's nothing, absolutely nothing you can do about it, is there, my sweet one?'

He was gloating again and Lorraine knew she had fallen headlong into a trap, a man-trap, and she fought wildly to get free. 'Isn't there?' she cried. 'Isn't there? What about Matthew? How do you know I don't love *him*? He's a fine man. He's honest, he's loyal and above all, he's faithful.'

His eyes froze hard. 'Which I am not.'

'No, you're not. You told me so yourself.'

He looked at her in silence. His expression became calculating. 'You're so sure of that, so sure that Matthew's the faithful type.'

'I know he loves me,' she whispered.

'And you love him back?' Her eyes flickered and fell from his. His voice hardened. 'I know who you love, my sweet.' There was sarcasm, not warmth in the endearment. '*And it's not Matthew!*'

'He wants to marry me.' She whispered the words as though they were proof of Matthew's love.

The silence was full of his contempt. At last he said, 'You'd do that? You'd use Matthew to get me out of your system?' Then he smiled and it was a cynical, mirthless smile. 'Shame on you!' He walked out.

Lorraine turned her face to the pillow and buried her burning cheeks in its softness. Now she knew. Deliberately and in cold blood he had made her love him. Deliberately he had set out to make her emotionally dependent on him, just to prove to himself that he could do it. And she had let it happen. Against her better judgement, she had come to trust him, and she knew now that she would regret it for the rest of her life.

Some time later she heard Matthew say, 'What's wrong, love?' She lifted her face from the pillow and turned on to her back, letting him see her tears.

When he took her in his arms she sobbed uncontrollably and clung to him, as he stroked her hair and tried to soothe her.

The door opened. Alan said, 'Lorraine, I've brought you some newspapers to——' but she held on to Matthew as if she would never let him go.

Neither of them turned to look at Alan and he went out, clicking the door shut behind him. The sound was terse and final.

Matthew asked her why she was crying. When she told him he shook his head. 'You take him too seriously, love. He doesn't mean half of what he says. He loves words. He has to, in his job.'

'But he meant it, I know he did,' she insisted.

He shrugged. 'In that case, the best thing for you to do is to put him out of your mind, isn't it?'

She smiled weakly. 'I suppose you're right. I'll try to do as you say.'

Alan's mother extended her visit until the New Year. She was good company and she often talked of Alan as a boy. Lorraine found both pleasure and pain in listening to her stories. Then Beryl would join in with tales about Lorraine as a little girl. Alan, who had all his meals downstairs while his mother was there, would listen and comment disinterestedly when appealed to by the others.

It was New Year's Eve and Alan left them about ten o'clock. He had a press engagement and could not say what time he would be home.

'Not till the small hours?' queried Matthew, who was sitting with his arm round Lorraine.

'Perhaps not even then,' Alan answered, his eyes dwelling maliciously on Lorraine. 'It depends on how—er—involved I get.'

Lorraine steeled herself not to react at all to his words, except to move closer to Matthew. Alan said goodnight to his mother, then to the others, and threw a mocking smile in Lorraine's direction. He went out, slamming the door behind him.

James had joined them for the evening and they watched the television programme and when midnight came and the New Year was born, they toasted each other and sang 'Auld Lang Syne.'

Lorraine did not hear Alan come home. She met him on the stairs next morning. He was in his dressing gown and on his way to the bathroom. He looked heavy-eyed and irritable. Lorraine pretended to look surprised to see him and he said caustically, 'Yes, I came home after all. I didn't stay out all night. Disappointed, because I acted out of character?'

Lorraine replied, her tone renouncing all possible claim to the emotion, 'Disappointed? What, *me*?' She shook her head. 'I had Matthew, so I was perfectly content. No, if anyone is disappointed it must be you. Obviously the New Year didn't come up to your expectations. Or are you losing your powers of persuasion where the opposite sex is concerned?' She swept past him, having the satisfaction of seeing him grind his teeth at what she had said.

The following day, Alan's mother went home. She embraced Lorraine and kissed her warmly. 'You must come and stay with me some time soon, my dear. I don't want it to be another ten years before I see you again. Get Alan to bring you during the school holidays.'

Lorraine promised to put aside a few days in the summer. 'But I'd travel by train,' she added. 'I wouldn't bother Alan.'

Nancy frowned. 'It wouldn't be a bother, would it, Alan?'

'Bother?' His eyes turned to Lorraine and mocked her. 'No, it would be no bother, but it wouldn't be advisable, would it? After all, I might run out of petrol, then who knows what might happen? Remember that I'm one of those low newspaper types, and we all know what Lorraine thinks of them.'

His mother laughed. 'He's only fooling, Lorraine. Of

155

course he'll bring you.'

'I wouldn't be too sure of that.' Lorraine looked at him swiftly, searching his face in vain for something to take the sting out of his words. 'By the summer,' he went on, 'circumstances might have altered radically.'

His mother looked anxious. 'If you mean by that statement that you're contemplating marriage, son, at least let me see the girl once before she becomes my daughter-in-law.'

'I think I can promise you that, Mother—if and when it happens.' He urged her gently towards the door.

Lorraine tried to hide her misery. 'So he's going to marry Margot, after all,' she thought. 'Some time soon, probably, when Margot's ready.'

After that, Matthew became even more protective, particularly when Alan was around, and Lorraine found it pleasing and comforting to bask in his show of affection.

When the new term began at school, she continued with the project of newspapers. She talked about it in the staff room to Ann and some of the others overheard. One of them was Miss Grimson, the senior English teacher.

'You are quite wrong to do this, Miss Ferrers,' she said severely. 'I've told you before, it's not in the syllabus, therefore you are, in my opinion, grossly wasting the girls' time on such a frivolous subject.' She stalked away and Ann grinned.

'Watch out, Lorraine. If you're not careful, you'll find yourself growing like her.' She looked at Lorraine's hair which she was wearing tied tightly back again.

Lorraine glanced at Miss Grimson who was sitting across the other side of the room drinking her third cup of tea. Her hair, grey and lifeless, was tugged tightly into a bun which rested against the nape of her neck. Her parchment-like skin was creased with frown marks. Her eyes, with the darting, sneaking criticism which never left them, were windows on the orthodox rigidity of her mind.

156

'Never,' said Lorraine, 'never will I get like that.'

'All the same, you're on your way. Your disappointment in love is showing, dear. Take warning—if you let yourself get sour, that's how you'll be.'

A few days later, Lorraine had a summons from the headmistress. She told Ann at morning break.

'It's that Grimson creature,' said Ann. 'They're friends, Lorraine, and she's been telling tales. Have your answers ready. Don't let the old dragon get you down.'

As Lorraine took her seat opposite the headmistress and looked at her puffy chin and cold eyes, she knew that Ann's description of her as an 'old dragon' did not go far enough. She was short and short-tempered and swelled out in all the wrong places. 'Only two more years,' the younger teachers would sigh, 'then the old battleaxe retires.'

Miss Mallady turned sharp eyes to Lorraine. 'I hear, Miss Ferrers, that you're wilfully breaking the rules and ignoring the syllabus in the teaching of your subject.'

Lorraine roused herself to reply in fighting tones. 'That is not strictly true, Miss Mallady. I'm adhering to the syllabus, but I'm introducing extra material which I consider relevant to the teaching of modern English.'

'In what way, may I ask?'

'In the context of modern times, of present-day needs and bearing in mind the changing patterns of the English language. I've chosen the subject of newspaper production because I think it best illustrates these things to the girls and because it lets them know what is going on in the world outside the academic atmosphere of the school.'

'So you set yourself up as an authority on the subject? From what source have you obtained your information?'

'I've read books about it, and I—I have a journalist acquaintance who——'

'A *journalist*?' Miss Mallady made it a word of abuse. 'I might have known.' She looked at Lorraine as though she had just claimed friendship with a hardened criminal. 'I

157

must ask you formally, Miss Ferrers, to abandon this non-sense. You are upsetting the other teachers in the English department with your upstart ideas. The girls will learn soon enough of the temptations of the outside world. Until then they must be protected in every possible way. We must preserve the academic traditions of this old-established school in the face of the gross distractions and temptations of present-day life.'

Lorraine raised her eyes over the other woman's head and gazed for a moment at the large portrait of Queen Victoria which hung in isolated splendour over the fire-place. She realised fully what she was up against.

'Two more years,' she told herself, as she dragged her feet along the corridor to the staff room. 'Only two more years before she retires.' But it still seemed an eternity.

That evening, after taking her class at the technical college, Lorraine returned home tired and dispirited. She had been worrying about her discussion with the headmistress and wished she knew what to do. It would have helped to talk to someone. She would have liked to ask Alan's advice, but there had been virtually no communication between them for days. Lorraine had kept out of his way whenever it was humanly possible to do so and he seemed to be repaying the compliment in good measure. Then she thought of Matthew—he would listen. He would be sympathetic even if he couldn't advise.

She took off her coat and hung it in the hall cupboard. She heard voices from Alan's room, but there was nothing unusual about that. She wondered unhappily if he was entertaining another of his 'flowers'. Then she froze where she stood. She knew now who was Alan's guest. It was Matthew, and it was his laughter she could hear. But it was not that which had made her go cold. It was the sound of Margot's voice, high-pitched, over-excited, in full cry after another man, another conquest. She was pursuing new quarry—and that quarry was Matthew.

Alan's voice came back, taunting, sarcastic, 'So you're sure,' he had said, 'so sure that Matthew's the faithful type?' Even as he had spoken the words he must have been working out, in his cold calculating way, a method of taking him from her.

And he knew by past experience just how to put Matthew's faithfulness to the test, the test of Margot's charms. So the vicious circle was still turning, it was all happening again. Margot and Hugh, Margot and Matthew.

Lorraine was caught up in a storm of anger, searing violent, terrifying anger. But like the swift, destructive tornado that it was, it passed almost as quickly as it had come, lifting her and dashing her down, leaving her beached and played out on the shifting sands of her own inadequacies. She realised then the inevitability of it all.

She went into the lounge and sat, limp and tired, in the armchair. James was reading the paper and her mother was heating some milk in the kitchen.

James lowered his paper and greeted her quietly. He raised his paper again and continued with his reading. Lorraine stared hopelessly into the fire. There was silence for a long time. She heard James lower the newspaper and fold it carefully. Lorraine knew he was looking at her.

'Don't let your heartbreak show so much, my dear,' he said softly. 'It not only spoils your looks, it might spoil your chances.'

She raised her eyes dully, surprised at the accuracy of his thought-reading.

'It isn't Matthew, is it, as your mother and I had hoped?'

'I'm sorry,' she said simply.

He laughed briefly, leaned back, hiding his disappointment. 'Just one of those things.'

She looked at his compassionate face and knew she could talk to this kindly man her mother had chosen to marry. She could talk to him as she had never been able to talk to

159

her own father. Although she had been so fond of him and was so like him in personality and character, he had, with his stiff unyielding attitude to life kept her and everyone else at bay, even his own wife who, with her warm and affectionate nature must have suffered some unhappiness.

But James had a warmth which drew like a magnet. 'Today,' Lorraine began slowly, 'I had some trouble at school.' And she unburdened herself to him and felt all the better for it.

'It's Alan's influence, isn't it? Alan who's changed your outlook and your ideas?'

'What's wrong with changing one's ideas?' she asked, on the defensive.

'Nothing, my dear, except that, now you appear to be on your own, without Alan's moral support, you must be one hundred per cent certain in your own mind that you have the necessary conviction and strength of purpose to follow these ideas through—alone.'

Lorraine scarcely hesitated. 'I have.'

'Good. Then carry on and I wish you the best of luck. You'll probably need it.'

'Now that's something,' she said tearfully, 'which seems to have been evading me lately.'

He smiled. 'It'll all come right in the end.'

'You sound just like my mother. You've caught her undaunted optimism.'

He smiled fondly. 'That's one of the reasons why I love her.'

Lorraine stared at him. That any other man could love her mother as her late father had done had not really penetrated the surface of her mind. In that moment she grew up a little. She realised that before long she and her mother would have to part and go their own separate ways. Her mother would belong to James and she, Lorraine, would have to make her own way through life, alone.

Beryl brought in the hot drinks and while they drank

them, she chatted to James and Lorraine listened to the laughter and the noise overhead. It was late when Matthew put his head round the door. He raised his hand to his father and went across to Lorraine. He bent over her as she sat in the armchair and kissed her on the cheek instead of the lips as he usually did. She remembered Hugh and his bird-like pecks and felt with silent misery that history was repeating itself.

'Tired, love?' Matthew asked with brotherly affection.

She nodded. 'Enjoying yourself up there?' She tried to keep the rancour out of her voice.

'I am, yes. I'm glad Alan invited me to meet her. She's a grand girl, Margot. Ever met her?'

Lorraine's eyes closed down and she knew he was too besotted to notice. 'Yes.'

'Come on up, then, and join in. I'm sure Alan won't mind.'

'No, thanks.' She couldn't hide her sourness now. 'I've no wish to watch another of my boy-friends being enticed away.'

She saw the shaft of pain which shot through him—but there was something else, the sort of half-hidden predatory determination which one sees in a man who has fallen headlong for a woman and will allow no criticism, nothing, to alter his views of her. She had seen it all before in Hugh.

Matthew patted her on the shoulder and returned upstairs. She told herself that she knew when she was beaten. She had come to terms at last with her own personality. Now she acknowledged without question that she had nothing permanent to offer any man, nothing to hold his interest for more than a short length of time.

She stared into the fire and the yellow flames stretched and curled and turned into molten gold before her brimming eyes.

'You've lost him, Lorrie, you've lost Matthew.' It was

James' quiet, kindly voice using her mother's pet name for her. 'And in the circumstances, my dear, you can't blame him.'

She shook her head. 'I'm not blaming him,' her voice sounded thick and she pressed her lips together. 'It's me, that's all. I'm the one at fault. I sent him away. Somehow, I send them all away.'

She saw her mother and James exchange glances like a couple who had been married for years and that served to make her even more aware of the fact that she was already shut out of their lives. She was now, even before their marriage, on her own. As indeed she always would be.

CHAPTER X

LORRAINE reverted to her old careless ways of dressing. She had stopped using make-up and she had stopped caring. At school she looked at Miss Grimson, with her disappointed eyes and the bitter tightness of her lips. 'Watch out,' Ann had said, 'you'll get like that.' Lorraine accepted that now, but she didn't care any more.

She had put a wall between Alan and herself and she was determined that never again would he break his way through her defences. Not that he tried. She decided that he had given her up. They barely exchanged smiles. 'He doesn't exactly cut me dead,' Lorraine reflected, 'but it's the nearest thing to it.'

At school they were working hard for Open Day. Despite the headmistress's warning, Lorraine pressed on with the newspaper project and the girls were putting together a fine display for the exhibition in the classroom.

Miss Grimson tackled her again about it. 'I thought you had been given instructions by the headmistress to abandon this nonsense?'

'I assure you, Miss Grimson, that when Open Day is over, I shall be giving up the whole idea and after that keeping strictly to the syllabus.'

What she did not tell her was that the fight had gone out of her and that without Alan's backing and moral support, nothing seemed worth while any more.

One evening in mid-February, Alan caught Lorraine on the landing. She looked at him, really looked at him for the first time for weeks and saw in his face some signs of strain. She was surprised and, loving him as she did, a little worried.

'That Christmas present I gave you,' he said, and although he spoke half jokingly he seemed on edge, 'it must still be in mint condition.'

She looked at him inquiringly and he went on, 'Your record—the New World Symphony, it's never been played, has it?' She shook her head. 'Would you object then,' he asked, 'if I borrowed it? I'd love to hear it again.'

'Of course you can borrow it.' She went into her bedroom, found the record and handed it to him.

'Come in and listen to it, Lorraine. You like it too, don't you? That's why I bought it for you.'

There was something in his eyes which stopped the refusal in her throat. She knew she would have to stay because it would have seemed so ungrateful to do otherwise. He pointed to an armchair and she sat down. She lost herself and her unhappiness in the beauty of the music. When it was over she opened her eyes and saw in his face as he looked at her such deep compassion that she nearly cried out.

'So he's sorry for me,' she thought, 'he pities me.' It made the pain she was enduring inside her even harder to bear. She began to rise, but he said, 'No, stay there.'

He leaned back in his chair and idly took something from his pocket to fiddle with. It was a penknife and he absent-mindedly flicked it open and shut.

'Lorraine,' he said, then hesitated, appearing to choose his words, 'I'm sorry about what has happened.' He saw her puzzled look. 'About Matthew and Margot. But,' he stopped and seemed to force himself to go on, 'you have to realise, as indeed we all do, that because you love someone, it doesn't necessarily mean that they will love you back.' Lorraine had the odd feeling that he was talking to himself as well as to her—did he have his own love for Margot in mind? she wondered. 'I mean,' he ran his finger lightly up and down the blades, 'your love for them doesn't give you the automatic right to their love.'

His eyes lifted at last and sought hers. 'I saw you at Christmas in Matthew's arms and it was only then that I realised how much you loved him.'

She shook her head helplessly, wanting to speak, to explain, to shout out, 'It's you I love, not Matthew. And I know, I have accepted, that you don't love me back.'

He watched her narrowly, apparently assessing her reaction, then he returned to flicking the penknife, feeling the blades. He said at last, in an odd speculative voice,

'If there were anything I could do to alter the situation——' The knife slipped, he cut himself and flung the penknife down with a curse. She ran across to him and gasped at the depth of the cut. He fumbled for his handkerchief and pressed it over the wound to stem the flow of blood.

'Wash it, Alan,' she cried, 'wash it in the bathroom. The blade was probably dirty.'

He looked up into her face, saw the anxiety and pain—his pain—reflected there and he laughed. He threw himself back in the armchair and laughed.

'You care, you really care, don't you? I've got through to you again. I've brought you back to life. My God, I thought I'd never manage it!'

She lost her temper. 'You did it for the purpose, didn't you? It was a rotten, dirty trick...'

'Don't be an idiot, woman. No one in his right mind would cut himself for the purpose. But it did the trick, it did the trick.' He was still gloating. He leaned forward and seized her hand, but she tried to pull away.

He jerked her down and on to his knee. 'Sit there,' he said. 'Sit there and pacify me. Soothe me, that's all I want, nothing else. Good God, you're a woman and I'm a man, and I need some womanly sympathy. I've cut myself. I've lost Margot. You've lost Matthew. Let's pacify each other.'

So she stayed there, secretly delighting in the touch of him, not caring that once again he only wanted her there as a substitute for Margot. She was used to the role by now and accepted it as gladly as a starving man accepts a handful of crumbs because it satisfied, for a time, her longing for him.

She stretched out her hand and touched his tie. 'You're wearing my present again. You've worn it a lot, haven't you?'

'So you've noticed?' He smiled and lowered his head to touch her hand with his lips. She flushed with pleasure.

'Why, Alan?'

'Because it's the best-quality tie I possess,' he said.

Bitterly disappointed, she took her hand away and clasped her fingers tightly on her lap.

He asked her, 'How's school these days?'

She told him that she had got into touble with the headmistress and had decided that after Open Day she would give up the newspaper project. Her enthusiasm had gone, she told him, but she didn't say why. He was sympathetic and understanding and tried to persuade her to change her mind. He laughed derisively at the headmistress's Victorian attitude.

'So your open day's next week, is it? Where's my diary?' He fumbled in his pocket and handed the diary to her. 'You make a note of it for me. I can't write with this damned sore finger.'

She wrote, under the appropriate date, 'Open Day at Lorraine's school,' feeling absurdly pleased that he had allowed her access to such a private possession as his diary. 'There, can you read it?'

He nodded. 'Written in a firm and rounded hand.' His eyes dallied over her. 'Like the rest of you.' He snapped the diary shut and put it away. 'I'll get a man to report it.'

'I don't think you should, Alan,' she said, and told him of Miss Mallady's sanctimonious horror of journalists.

He patted her on the back and pushed her off his knee. 'Don't worry, the man I send will be able to cope with a horde of Miss Malladys. Now it's time I bandaged this mortal wound.' He went into the bathroom to wash it, then Lorraine applied healing cream and adhesive plaster.

He looked down at her as she tended his thumb. 'I should be eternally grateful to that penknife of mine. It brought Sleeping Beauty back to life.' She smiled and he said quickly, 'Hold that smile while I get my camera and snap it. After all, it might never happen again.'

She laughed and felt as though a mountain had slipped from her shoulders.

The school authorities chose the town's early closing day to open its doors to parents and relatives. The trickle of visitors began at two o'clock and increased as the afternoon progressed. All the time, Lorraine was on duty in the classroom which displayed the work on the newspaper project.

On large sheets of paper which were pinned to the wall they had placed, side by side, different versions of the same story which had been reported by several newspapers. There were conflicting headlines, there were phrases ringed and underlined revealing policy differences and drawing attention to the slant on reports which showed up the bias of the newspaper proprietors.

They had shown how the same story could be given headline treatment in one paper, only to be tucked away in a small paragraph on the inside page of another.

There were displays of news photographs over the walls and a description with illustrations of how a newspaper is put together.

Lorraine was wandering round the exhibits and watching the girls at work when a tall, self-assured young man walked in. 'Miss Ferrers? My name's Mills of the *Walkley Evening Press.*'

They shook hands. 'I take it Mr. Darby sent you?'

'That's right. He said there would be something here of interest to us, something about a project on newspapers.'

He looked around. 'I suppose this is what he was talking about?' She nodded. 'Mind if I wander about and make a few notes?'

'Go ahead,' she invited, 'as long as what you say is accurate and fair and that you don't give more prominence to what I've done than to other teachers' efforts.' Then she asked, 'I take it you have seen the headmistress?'

He had already started making notes and seemed preoccupied. 'I called into the headmistress's office on my way in.' He stopped writing. 'By the way, I've got a photographer with me. You don't object if we take one or two pictures of your display?' He smiled persuasively. 'It's all in the interests of better relations between ourselves and the public.'

Lorraine replied that as long as it was all right with Miss Mallady, she didn't mind. The photographer came in and she recognised him as the man who had seen Alan and herself dining together at the Pine Needles just before Christmas. This was the man, she remembered, who had annoyed Alan so much.

He shook her by the hand and said he recognised her from their other meetings. He took a few pictures of the display, then he looked at his colleague and raised his eyebrows. It must have been a prearranged signal because the reporter stopped writing and said,

'What we should like to do, if you're willing, Miss Ferrers, is to take a picture of you standing at the blackboard with some chalk in your hand, as though you were taking a lesson. We could feature the photograph alongside the report. Would you mind posing for us?'

The idea worried her, but she told them that as long as the headmistress approved, she would do as they asked. She assumed that Alan had known what he was about in sending them both and she allowed them to take the photograph. They seemed pleased, thanked her for her co-operation and left the school.

The last of the visitors drifted away about five o'clock and Lorraine met Ann as they were going home. 'How did it go?' Ann asked.

Lorraine told her about the two men from Alan's newspaper and she seemed surprised that Alan had thought it worth while sending them.

Lorraine explained that she knew that they were coming.

'He sent a photographer too, did he?' said Ann. 'That's unusual, isn't it? I suppose they got old Mallady's permission?'

'They said they had, although she must have had a change of heart since she last spoke to me. She gave me the impression that she considered newspapermen to be less than the dust.'

Alan was on his way out that evening when Lorraine met him in the hall. 'How did Open Day go?' he asked.

'Very well, thanks,' she told him, but did not elaborate as he seemed to be in a hurry.

At school next day they dismantled the exhibits and displays and stored them in drawers and cupboards.

After tea Lorraine left to take her evening class at the technical college. She hurried home, hoping to see Alan and ask him to let her see a copy of his paper. She assumed there would be a report in it of the school open day. But he was out and did not return until after she had gone to bed. As he always left the house immediately after an early breakfast, she missed him again, so it was not until she arrived at the school that the storm broke over her head.

Miss Grimson stood in the staff-room doorway. Her arms were folded, her face was flushed and her eyes were rolling in outrage.

'Miss Ferrers!' she bawled, although she stood only a few feet away, 'you are wanted at once by the headmistress.'

Lorraine said, as calmly as she could, 'Do you mind if I put my things on the desk first?'

With bad grace Miss Grimson moved so that she could

pass and then stood over her like a prison warder, determined to allow her no chance to escape. The other teachers stared at Lorraine, some with pity, some with distaste. Ann walked across to her, shaking her head.

'You've done it now, dearie. You've got it coming.'

'Got what coming?' Lorraine hissed back.

'I'm surprised at Alan,' Ann went on, 'surprised he allowed it.'

'Allowed what, for goodness' sake?' Lorraine asked, feeling worried now.

But Ann had no time to reply. Miss Grimson's voice boomed from the doorway, 'Miss Ferrers, the headmistress must not be kept waiting.'

With anxiety dragging at her feet and her brain moving in circles trying to find a reason for all the mystery, she went to Miss Mallady's study. Miss Grimson followed close behind, probably to make certain, Lorraine thought, with a humourless smile, that she was delivered safely into enemy hands.

As Lorraine knocked and entered, the close atmosphere of the headmistress's study had her by the throat. She was sure that Miss Grimson remained outside to listen in on the conversation.

But conversation, Lorraine thought ruefully, was hardly the correct description for what took place. Miss Mallady charged into her verbally, like a raging bull, and battered her almost senseless with her abuse before Lorraine could grasp what she was trying to say.

'Disgusting!' she hurled across the desk. 'A blow to the school's fine and ancient tradition of learning! You deserve to be sacked, sent packing on the spot. Shameless,' she raged, 'wicked! You're not fit to be a member of the teaching profession!'

Lorraine listened to the speaker and watched her gesticulating with self-righteous fury. She saw it all with a becalmed numbness. Her ignorance of what the headmistress

170

was talking about protected her like a suit of armour. She stood there stunned but dispassionately amused.

When the speaker paused for breath, Lorraine asked mildly, 'If you would just explain what you're talking about——'

The headmistress drew in a gasp of air. 'Are you trying to tell me that you do not know what I am referring to?'

'Not at all, I'm afraid.' Lorraine shook her head to add emphasis to the words.

Miss Mallady opened a drawer, took out a newspaper—Alan's newspaper—and spread it roughly on the desk so that Lorraine could read it. She pointed to the centre of the front page.

It was some minutes before Lorraine could fully take in what she was looking at. She stared, not wanting to believe what her eyes were telling her. She saw, in front of her, two pictures of herself set side by side and enlarged out of all proportion to their importance.

One showed her at the blackboard, chalk in hand, in front of the class. The other was a snapshot of her in the garden at home, lying full-length and wearing the two-piece swimsuit she had bought for her summer holiday with Ann in the Scilly Isles.

The caption ran, 'Lorraine Ferrers, attractive young schoolteacher, makes the girls take notice at school and the boys sit up and take notice at home.'

She felt the colour drain from her face. She groped for a chair that wasn't there. She could not believe that this had happened to her. In despair her mind cried out, 'How?' She forced herself to recall in detail that warm, lazy afternoon in September.

Alan had gone out, then returned home. Before joining her in the garden, he must have gone up to his room, looked out of the window and seen her sunbathing. He must have put a special lens on his camera and photographed her as she lay there on the tartan rug.

171

She remembered the odd sound she had heard, like a window closing, and at the time, she had concluded that it was someone next door.

Trying to clear her eyes, Lorraine attempted to read the article alongside the pictures. The writer had set out, in excruciating detail, the scope and aims of the project. He had been lavish in his praise of what he called the teacher's 'missionary zeal' in trying to bridge the gap between the schools and the much-misunderstood world of journalism.

He said that her efforts 'shone like a light in a dark tunnel' when taken in the context of the school she worked in. She blushed with embarrassment and understood now only too well the cause of the headmistress's outrage.

Miss Mallady sat there relishing Lorraine's discomfiture and in her moment of victory became almost benign to the vanquished. She took up the paper and folded it with elaborate care and, turning her head away as though she could not bear the sight of it, dropped it into the waste-paper basket.

'I trust you will now admit that you have made an unpardonable blunder in allowing this to happen, and that you realise that your place as a teacher in this school is scarcely tenable after this disgraceful episode.'

'No doubt you will not believe me, Miss Mallady,' Lorraine said, 'but I was not responsible.' Her voice faltered and fell. Her defiance, her will to oppose and to uphold her own principles had been annihilated by the anguish which laid waste her feelings at the thought of the treachery of the man who was to blame for what had happened. 'I was as ignorant as you were that anything like this would be published. I made a point of asking the reporter if he had got your permission, and I understood that he had.'

'He did no such thing!' Miss Mallady bellowed, her condescension wiped out by such an outrageous attack on her integrity. 'All he did was to call into my study. I was absent, but my secretary saw him and told him to look for me and obtain my permission. Needless to say, he did not find me, no doubt knowing that I would have given him a dusty answer and sent him packing.'

Having avenged her professional honour, she relaxed into a show of magnanimous disbelief. 'In any case, my dear Miss Ferrers,' her tone made a mockery of the two words preceding Lorraine's surname, 'you cannot possibly hope to persuade me of your innocence. You must have posed for the photographer in front of the blackboard. You must likewise have posed for the photographer in that—in that—position in the garden.'

Lorraine shook her head helplessly, but the headmistress swept on, 'You entertained,' she gave the word all the dubious overtones of immorality she could muster, 'a reporter in the classroom on Open Day. You are surely not trying to tell me that you are so unworldly as to think that a reporter attends any function merely for the good of his health?'

Lorraine knew that her sarcasm was meant to shrivel her up, but it passed over her head. Nothing could touch her now. Alan had turned traitor. True to his profession, he had proved that he was capable of throwing anyone to the wolves, whether friend or foe, if such an action could further his interests.

'I think,' the headmistress was saying, 'you would be best advised to apply for a teaching post in other schools. I cannot see how, after this affair, we can retain the trust of the parents of our girls if you remain on the staff. Add to this the fact,' she droned on, and Lorraine was scarcely listening, 'that the contents of the article reveal that you continued, quite against my wishes, to deal with a subject which was not in the syllabus, then I can find no extenuating circumstances which might exonerate you from blame.' She dismissed Lorraine with a wave of the hand.

As the day dragged by, Lorraine found that it was not the headmistress's words which tortured her, nor was it the attitude of the majority of the staff, who treated her as if she had an infectious disease. It was the thought of Alan's treachery which hurt so deeply that she wanted to cry out with pain.

Ann's anxious sympathy acted as a temporary balm. But it was Hugh's condescending smile as he wandered up to her saying, 'You've made a spectacle of yourself, haven't you, Lorraine? One of Alan's little jokes?' which lit the fuse of her anger. And when she opened the front door and found her mother greeting her with a happy smile, holding out the *Walkley Evening Press*, she vented all her horded spleen on her.

'But, dear,' Beryl wailed, visibly ducking under the full force of her daughter's words, 'they're such lovely pictures of you.'

'All I want,' Lorraine raged, 'is maternal pride flung at me now! Shall I tell you what my precious headmistress said to me?' She didn't wait for an answer, she told her mother in detail.

When she paused to gather verbal reinforcements, Beryl frowned and murmured, 'I wish James was here. He'd calm you down.'

'No one could calm me down,' Lorraine shouted. 'No one!'

When she saw the tears in her mother's eyes, she stopped. She had passed her pain on to her and she could have kicked herself. She sat down, put a hand to her throbbing head and said, 'I suppose your paying guest is out as usual? I suppose he feels he can't face me after this. No wonder he's been avoiding me for the last day or so. He knew what was coming, didn't he?'

'Don't condemn him, dear, until he's had his say.'

'Condemn him? What else am I supposed to do? Fling my arms round his neck and thank him for practically losing me my job?'

174

'*I* don't think Alan did it, Lorrie. He's not that sort of boy.'

'Don't give me that, Mum. Of course he did it. It made a good story and he knew it. No journalist could resist a good story, no matter who's involved. He's no different from his—his confederates. He's got no ethics, any more than they have.'

'Don't talk about him like that, Lorrie. He's Nancy Darby's boy.' Lorraine could hear the tears in her mother's voice again. Beryl went on shakily, 'Anyway, it wouldn't do you any harm to change schools. I always did say that Mallady woman was an old haybag. You've been getting like them, Lorrie. I told you, didn't I? I was getting so worried about you, you were growing all prim and proper. This could be the saving of you. Find a nice new school with a young headmistress and nice new ideas.'

Her mother's lack of sympathy was the flash-point. She jerked herself out of the chair and shouted, 'I'm going out!'

'But, Lorrie, it's teatime now and James is coming for me soon.'

'I couldn't eat a thing.'

'And it looks like rain.'

'Let it rain!' She ran upstairs, changed into old trousers and flung on her windcheater. She went downstairs, put her head round the door and said, 'When your beloved paying guest comes in you can tell him——' to her annoyance her voice wavered, 'just what I think of him.'

She slammed out of the house. She knew where she was going—to her sanctuary. She caught the bus and got out at the usual place. She started walking. The damp smell of the undergrowth was redolent and heady and suggestive of happier times which, corroded as she was with anger, she had no wish to recall. She walked so fast she was gasping for breath when she reached the top. She had no desire to look around and savour the view. It mean nothing to her now.

She sat under a tree, feeling the dampness beneath her. Rain had started falling steadily. It came through the leafless, lifeless branches on to the hood which she pulled over her head. The February afternoon was brooding and chill. Despite the creeping dampness which stiffened her limbs, she tried to compose herself and bring some order to the chaos of her emotions.

This was her hideaway, she told herself, her refuge. Now she could set about finding herself again. But not any more, it seemed. She found she could not escape the problems she had gone up there to solve. Problems? she thought. No, problem, singular. Alan. It was Alan she was running from, nothing else, and he was there with her, haunting her, invisible but at her side.

She drew up her legs and hugged them, resting her forehead on her knees. She tried to think, to cut a path through her anger and see her way forward into the future. She would change her job and she would leave home. She could not continue to live in the same house as that—that traitor.

Soon her mother would marry James, and they planned to buy a new house. They had invited her to live with them, but she would not go. She would do what others of her age had done—find a flat or digs. Alan? His plans probably included Margot who would no doubt leave Matthew as she had left all the other men who had temporarily attracted her. She would return to her real love, Alan Darby.

There were footsteps striding up the hill, regular, determined, familiar footsteps. It was almost dark now, and raining heavily. Lorraine peered into the gloom, straining her ears. They were firm and indomitable, those footsteps, and they knew where they were going. They were coming straight towards her.

CHAPTER XI

THE shadow of a shape formed into the figure of a man, a tall man who stopped in front of her and gazed down with hard, merciless eyes.

'I thought I'd find you here.'

She tightened like a tigress that had spotted its prey. 'You,' she breathed, 'why don't you leave me alone? I want to be left alone, most of all by you.'

He stood, silent and scarcely breathing.

She wanted to hurt him. 'Will you go? Will you stop tormenting me? Haven't you done enough damage, enough to keep you supplied with after-dinner stories until you're an old man? Well, all right, you've had your little joke. Now go!' Her voice was raised and ragged.

'Listen to me, Lorraine.' He spoke quietly and seemed sure, so sure that she would do as he asked. 'I want to explain——'

'Listen? To you? Listen to more of your lies? Let you provoke me into saying something else you can twist and slant and angle and splash across the front page of your gutter of a newspaper, with the sole aim of pushing up the circulation?'

'Have you finished?' he asked almost gently.

'No!'

'Right.' He eased himself down beside her, as heedless as she was of the dangerous dampness of the earth. 'I can wait. Carry on with your tirade.'

She hugged her knees even tighter. She had to have something to cling to, to act as a stabiliser. 'Yes, I will carry on. I'll let you into a secret, a secret that will probably make you crow with triumph. I'll tell you just what you've done to me since you came into my life. You've——

you've torn me apart. You've made me lonely, unbearably, *consciously* lonely—I was lonely before, but I accepted it. Now I hate it. You've made me restless, you've stirred me from my unawakened state and taken away my emotional independence. You've deprived me, one by one, of my friends—first Hugh, then you tried to take Ann away, then Matthew.'

'Tell me,' he asked almost casually, 'what was Matthew to you?' Lorraine was silent. 'You loved him?' Still she did not answer. He raised his hand and forced her to turn her head and his hard seeking eyes found hers in the gloom. '*You loved him?*'

She jerked her head away. 'I haven't finished,' she went on harshly, ignoring his question. 'You took away from me the basic confidence of my old ideas and you tried to inject new ones in their place. And now I'm lost,' her voice splintered into tiny pieces and she had to whisper, 'I'm lost, utterly lost.' She swallowed and talked on relentlessly, tears straining through.

'You've ruined my reputation at school. I've been advised to find another job . . .' She turned on him then. 'You were at the bottom of this. You did it. It was your brain child, this crazy feature about me you splashed across the front page.'

'You're wrong, Lorraine, so wrong.' He stared into the darkness. 'I know you'll reject my explanation, but by the time I caught up with what was happening, events were irreversible. There was nothing I could do. Believe me, if I'd been able to stop the presses, I would have done.'

'You really expect me to believe that? To believe that your loyalties did not lie with your paper and your job? I wasn't born yesterday. What about that photo of me in the garden? Who else could have taken it but you?'

'I admit I took it.'

'Then admit also that you showed it to your colleagues and suggested to them that they use it as in fact they did.

Argue yourself out of that one!'

'All right, I will.' He pulled at the grass at his side and hesitated like someone about to make a shattering admission. 'I carried that photo of you in my wallet.'

Her head shot round. 'Why?'

He shrugged. 'Why? Why does a man usually carry the picture of a girl in his wallet?'

'I have no doubt,' she sneered, 'that my photograph was one of half a dozen which you produced periodically to impress your colleagues and let them know how many women you had at your beck and call. Your "flowers", you probably called them. After all, I was one of them, wasn't I? You told me so at Christmas.'

With an angry gesture he slipped his hand into his inside pocket and drew out his wallet. He flung it on the ground between them. 'Look inside. See how many girls' photographs I've got there.'

Lorraine stared at it. She stared at him. 'You'd allow me to look in your wallet?'

'Yes,' he sneered. 'I trust you more than you trust me.'

Her hand stretched out and he watched her pick it up. She felt the smoothness of the expensive leather, caught the smell of the cigarette smoke which clung to it. It was so much part of him that she had the ridiculous desire to put it to her lips. Then it came to her why he was allowing her to inspect it. She threw it down as though it were burning her fingers.

'Of course you're letting me look at it. You removed all the other pictures before you came out. Hid them in a drawer probably until it's safe to put them back.'

With an explosive movement he grasped his wallet, stuffed it back into his pocket and stood up. Lorraine had never seen him so angry.

He turned his fury upon her. 'Your venomous tongue is enough to turn syrup sour. You've already absorbed into your system enough of the tartness and vinegar of your revered and ancient colleagues to make you one of them. Be warned, my dear Miss Ferrers,' his bitter sarcasm hit her like a blow across the face, 'in looks, in manner, in ideas, in wilful mistrust and deafness to what you don't want to hear, in stunted emotions and sheer physical frustration you are almost a replica of those you work with.' He lashed her relentlessly with his tongue and because of the darkness he could not see the tears which were trickling down her cheeks. 'I have done you the courtesy of listening to you patiently. I have heard your tirade out. Yet you shut your ears to my explanations, my side of the story. You want to be alone? Right, I'm leaving you alone. You can keep your loneliness as far as I'm concerned for the rest of your life.'

She watched him walk away down the hill, through the trees and out of sight. '*And fare thee well, my only love, And fare thee well a while!*'

There was silence, except for the steadily falling rain on the brittle dead leaves around her, silence except for the feverish pounding of her heart.

She stared into the darkness. She had sent him away as she had sent away all the others. And this was the man she loved as she knew she would never love another. She stood up, felt her clothes clinging to her body and realised that she was soaked to the skin. But she didn't care—she ran, she slithered and slipped down the hill over the wet earth, stumbling now and then in the tangle of tree roots and undergrowth.

'*And I will come again, my love, Tho' 'twere ten thousand mile.*' She had to reach him. Before it was too late, she had to get to him. She saw his outline ahead of her. He was still in the woods, walking slowly, heavily, hands in pockets, coat collar turned up against the rain.

She called his name. He stopped and turned but did not move. He waited, motionless, watching her feel her way towards him. Now she was standing a few feet away and her heartbeats had her at their mercy. Her eyes strained to see his face and drew back defeated at its uncompromising hardness. His stony indifference walled up her groping efforts to escape from her habitual reticence and reserve.

'Well?' His voice was harsh and bitter.

She had to find a way, she had to break down his barriers and get through to him. After rejecting his attempts at reconciliation with such finality, she knew it was she who would have to make the first move.

'Well?' It came again, harsher than before, and now there was impatience in his voice.

She struggled to find the key, a word, a single word would do. He turned away sharply and, desperate to hold him back, she put her hand on his arm. She found the word.

'Alan?'

He turned back to her. 'Alan,' her voice wavered and whispered, 'don't go away. Please don't go.'

His curt answer rebuffed her and put her almost physically from him. 'Why? Give me one good reason why, after all you have said to me, I shouldn't go.' The barriers grew higher and even more difficult to surmount.

She stared at his face in the darkness and felt the rain falling, steadily, softly, mingling with the tears on her up-turned cheeks. Hopelessly she shook her head. 'Alan, oh, Alan!' she sobbed.

His hands stayed where they were, in his pockets. They did not stretch towards her as she thought they might. She forced her stiff lips to say his name again. 'Alan, I——' Her voice broke. She saw his dark, unyielding eyes and could say no more.

Slowly his hands moved. They lifted and gripped her shoulders. 'Say it,' he commanded, shaking her, 'say it. *Say it!*'

She turned her face up to his and catching her breath at the look in his eyes, she whispered that she loved him.

'My God!' he muttered, 'I thought I'd never get it out of you. I thought it would never come.'

Then he trapped her in his arms and she drowned in his kiss. The rain ran unheeded down their cheeks and into their mouths, and she wanted to give and give to him until he had taken all he desired of her giving.

'My darling, oh, my darling,' he said, 'my own Lorraine.' He whispered endearments. He unzipped her jacket and slipped his arms inside. 'Soon you must marry me. I want to make you my wife.' He whispered in her ear, 'Tell me again what you said that day on the hill. If you married and he was a good man——'

'I'd stay with him for life. I'll never forsake you, my darling,' she murmured, 'never, never . . .'

He kissed her again and again and they lost all sense of time. Later, much later, she caught his wrist and peered at his watch.

'You're right, my sweet,' he said. 'We must go home. I want to get near you. I can't do that here.'

'You've been doing nothing else for the past hour,' she laughed.

'That's what you think, my darling,' he answered. He took her hand and they ran the rest of the way to the car, parked at the roadside. They drove home and he pushed her in the front door and up the stairs.

'Get into something dry,' he said, 'and when I've changed, I'll make some coffee. Want any food?'

'Yes, please. I'm hungry. I didn't have any tea.' She coloured at the question in his eyes.

'Now I wonder why? All right, I'll make a few sandwiches.'

'You're very good,' she said, as they kissed on the landing.

'I'm not, you know,' he answered, with a smile. 'You just wait and see.'

She took off her wet clothes and, uncharacteristically,

left them in a pile on the floor. But, she told herself, she was doing so many things out of character suddenly, and it was a wonderful feeling.

She dried her hair and it fluffed out round her cheeks. She slipped into blue slacks and white long-sleeved sweater, and put on a light covering of make-up, then ran down the stairs and Alan was arranging sandwiches on a plate.

'The coffee smells delicious,' she remarked, standing by his side.

'Of course it does. Look who made it. Help me bring this stuff up to my room.'

He sat in the armchair and Lorraine perched on the arm of it, and passed him sandwiches and coffee. He made a facetious comment about having just acquired the services of a slave. She collected the empty cups and put them on a tray.

'Come here,' he ordered, 'we've been parted long enough.' He held out his arms, and she went into them willingly. The only light came from a table lamp near the window and the electric fire which glowed warm and bright on the rug. For a long time the only sound was the patter of rain against the windows.

'My darling,' he murmured as they pulled apart, 'are you in a fit state to listen to me, because I've got a lot to say that must be said if there's to be complete trust between us.'

'Alan, that photograph . . .'

He kissed her gently. 'I took it, sweetheart, because you looked so beautiful I couldn't resist it.' She shook her head. 'It's true, Lorraine. If you want to know, I was in love with you then. Oh yes, I was, so you can stop shaking your head like that. I carried that photo in my wallet so that I could look at you now and then and admire you like any man in love.' She held her breath. 'One day at work I was searching in my wallet for a stamp and your picture fell out. One of the others spotted it on the floor and picked it up. In no time at all, it was being passed round all the reporters in the room. They asked who it was and I had to tell them. They all remembered you from the time you called in for the key. Each one of those men inspected it, and one or two others who had drifted in, and when I got angry they handed it back. One of the photographers asked if he could make a block of it to use in the paper as a pin-up. He said he'd mention no names. Of course I refused.' He stopped and stroked her hair as she lay in his arms. 'One day, without my knowledge, they must have taken it from my wallet for a couple of days, made a block and put the picture back.'

'But how did they manage it without your finding out?'

'Well, sometimes I would go out of the room for a discussion with the editor, for instance, and leave my jacket on the back of my chair. They knew this and of course that made it easy for them. Since I didn't look at your picture every day—just the knowledge that it was there was sometimes sufficient,' she reached up and put a kiss on his cheek, which he returned, 'I didn't miss it. They heard about the open day at your school—I told them all about your project—and, being alert and well-trained reporters, they put one and one together and literally made two and a front page splash. I didn't instruct a photographer to go. He scented a story—don't forget he saw us dining together that night. They knew how annoyed I would have been if I'd known what was going on, so they cleverly kept it from me by devious methods until at last I had to see the finished version of the front page. By that time it was too late for me to do a thing about it. And I certainly didn't make up that caption to the pictures,' he smiled, 'although even you, Lorraine, must admit that it was a good one.'

He lowered his voice and pulled her closer. 'Sweetheart, it was that old, old conflict between love and duty. I knew what your reaction would be. I knew it would almost certainly get you into trouble, but my hands were tied. And when you wouldn't listen to me up there on the hill, I thought it was all over between us. Until I saw you running towards me——'

'Darling,' she said when they came back to earth, 'what about Margot?'

'Ah,' he said, smiling, and shifting her into a more comfortable position on his lap, 'I wondered when that was coming. Believe it or not, I've been trying to ditch Margot for months.'

Lorraine tugged herself upright. 'And you used my boyfriends to get rid of her?'

'Well, yes and no. But can you blame me if I did? It served a double purpose—at one stroke, it left the field clear for me where you were concerned and it also disposed of Margot.' He grinned provocatively. 'That night when she came and you were in my room, I tried to make you stay with me to show her that it was you I wanted. Unfortunately, my sweet, you wouldn't play ball. In true schoolmistress fashion you pushed your nose into the air and left me high and dry.'

'How was I to know what you were up to?' she asked, aggrieved.

'Darling, how could I tell you? I thought at the time that you loved Matthew.' He looked at her and frowned a little. 'Then I started to have my doubts. I was right to do so, wasn't I?'

She nodded. 'I didn't love Matthew. Liked him, but——'

'Admit it,' he interrupted with a smile, 'you've been in love with me for months, haven't you? You've fought me every inch of the way, you little minx.' He looked at her thoughtfully. 'Matthew and Margot—it's the real thing with them, did you know? They're madly in love.'

She raised her eyebrows, unable to believe it.

'It's true.' He rested his head on the back of the chair and said slowly, 'She's likeable, almost lovable, if you like 'em that way. In fact, the only thing wrong with Margot

185

was that she wouldn't leave me alone!'

They laughed together. 'You'll have to find another job, my darling. I can't have my wife made unhappy and miserable by——'

'By that old haybag, as my mother calls her.'

He laughed loudly, then became serious. 'I've been told, off the record, that there'll be a full-time lecturing job in English coming up soon at the technical college. Now,' he glanced at her provocatively, 'which one of us should apply? You or me? On second thoughts, it had better be you, because it's a junior position—hardly good enough for me!'

She opened her mouth to protest, but he closed it very effectively with his. When he had finished he said, 'When your mother marries James, we'll get a flat.' She sighed with contentment.

She put up her hand and straightened his tie—the tie she had given him for Christmas. Looking at it reminded her of a question which had been puzzling for some time now. She had to know the answer.

'Alan, if you weren't in love with Margot, who was the girl you came back early to see just after Christmas?'

'Why, you, you silly goose. Who else?' He looked down at her. 'Look at you, you shameless hussy, lying on me in this abandoned way. What would your pupils think? A dull, respectable schoolmarm like you—where's the stiff and starchy young woman who greeted me on the doorstep that day I came to live here?'

'She's gone for good, Alan, you've changed her beyond recognition. I don't know what you must have thought of me that day I opened the door to you.'

'Well, I'll tell you. In my job, we're trained to assess potential. You know what I mean? We're trained to look beneath the surface and see what "could be" as well as "what is." I looked beneath your "surface" and my word,' he grinned, 'with those flashing rebellious eyes and the challenge that shouted from every muscle of your body—

did you have potential !'

She laughed and asked him, 'What else were you thinking, darling, when you looked at me so oddly that day?'

'You really want to know?' She nodded. 'All right, I'll
tell you. She needs a man.'

She struggled indignantly, but he held her down.'Keep
still. Let me finish.' He said, smiling and indicating himself,
'This man.'

She turned her cheek to his and left it there. He went on
softly, 'And now you've got him—for life—whether you
want him or not.'

It took her quite a while to prove to him beyond all
shadow of doubt that she did want him—very much.

The front door opened and closed and a voice called,
'Lorrie? I'm home. Where are you, dear?'

Lorraine stirred sleepily. 'Alan darling, let's go and tell
my mother.'

He smiled as she scrambled off his lap and allowed her to
pull him upright. They walked on to the landing and looked
down at Beryl, who was gazing up at them with a puzzled
frown. For once she seemed lost for words.

'Hallo, Mum——' Lorraine began, but Alan swung her
round to face him. 'This will save words, and as a journalist, I love saving words,' and he pulled her close and
kissed her.

Beryl gave a strangled shriek of pure delight. '*My
darlings!*' she croaked, and dived up the stairs.

'Oh, my darlings,' she said again, stretching her arms
wide and encompassing them both. First she kissed Lorraine, then she kissed Alan, then she started all over again.

Her face was aglow and she asked excitedly, 'Alan, does
your mother know?'

'Not yet.' He smiled down at Lorraine. 'We've been
incommunicado for the past couple of hours.'

Beryl looked at her watch. 'I'm going to phone her.'

'But, Mum, it's nearly midnight!'

'I wouldn't care if it was three in the morning, I'd still phone her.'

She hurried down to the hall and dialled Nancy Darby's number. As she waited to be connected, she turned round and said, 'My darlings, I'm bewildered, I really am. I thought you didn't like each other. Do tell me, when did it all start?'

'Oh, that's easy,' Alan answered, looking into Lorraine's bright eyes, 'it all began—let me see—twenty-four years ago, when Lorraine was two and I was twelve . . .'

'Nancy? Listen, my dear, wonderful news. Lorrie and Alan—they're going to be married . . .'

Other titles available this month in the Mills & Boon Classics Series

3 specially chosen reissues of the best in Romantic Fiction

JAKE HOWARD'S WIFE
by Anne Mather

Jake Howard was immensely attractive, immensely rich, immensely successful. His wife Helen was beautiful, intelligent, well bred. A perfect couple, in fact, and a perfect marriage, everyone said. But everyone was wrong ...

A QUESTION OF MARRIAGE
by Rachel Lindsay

Beth was brokenhearted when Danny Harding let her down, and vowed that it would be a long time before she fell in love again. But fall in love again she did — with Danny's cousin Dean, a very different type of man indeed, and one who really loved her. Or did he? Surely fate wouldn't be so cruel as to strike Beth again in the same way?

WHISPERING PALMS
by Rosalind Brett

The discovery of mineral deposits on her African farm came just at the right time for Lesley, but besides prosperity, it brought a scheming sister determined to get most of the spoils herself and to marry the most eligible bachelor in Central Africa.

Mills & Boon Classics

— all that's great in Romantic Reading

Available October 1979

Titles available this month in the Mills & Boon ROMANCE Series

CHATEAU IN THE PALMS by *Anne Hampson*
Philippe de Chameral could have made Jane happy — but
he did not know that she was a married woman . . .

SAVAGE POSSESSION by *Margaret Pargeter*
Melissa had been too used to having her own way to allow
Ryan Trevelyan to dominate her — but she soon had to
change her tune!

ONE MORE RIVER TO CROSS by *Essie Summers*
Rebecca was as different from her flighty cousin Becky as
chalk from cheese, but the girls' identical appearance was to
get Rebecca into a difficult situation with the bossy Darroch . . .

LURE OF EAGLES by *Anne Mather*
An unknown cousin had inherited the family business, and
Domine found herself agreeing to the masterful Luis Aguilar's
suggestion that she accompany him to South America to meet
the girl.

MIDNIGHT SUN'S MAGIC by *Betty Neels*
Could Annis ever make Jake see that she had married him for
love, and not on the rebound?

LOVE IS A FRENZY by *Charlotte Lamb*
Seventeen-year-old Nicky Hammond's devotion was touching,
but Rachel couldn't possibly return it. Yet how could she
convince his disapproving father Mark that she wasn't cradle-
snatching — or worse?

THIS SIDE OF PARADISE by *Kay Thorpe*
Gina's so-called friend was after a man with money, so Gina
couldn't really blame Ryan Barras when he got entirely the
wrong idea about her . . .

A LAND CALLED DESERET by *Janet Dailey*
LaRaine had always been able to twist men round her finger
but, as luck would have it, she fell in love with Travis
McCrea — who had no time for her at all!

TANGLED SHADOWS by *Flora Kidd*
Kathryn could hardly refuse to return to her husband when
she learned from his family that he had lost his memory in
an accident — but would he remember what had destroyed
the marriage in the first place?

THE PASSIONATE WINTER by *Carole Mortimer*
Piers Sinclair was her boy-friend's father: older, more
sophisticated, far more experienced than she was. And so of
course Leigh fell in love with him . . .

Mills & Boon Romances
— all that's pleasurable in Romantic Reading!
Available October 1979

Forthcoming Classic Romances

WIFE FOR A PENNY
by Anne Hampson

If Liz didn't marry Nigel Shapani two family fortunes would
be lost, under the terms of an eccentric will. So she married
him, and he took her off to his home in Greece. But it was to
be a business arrangement only. She would never let herself
fall in love with him — to a Greek love, in a woman, meant
subservience, and Liz would never stand for that. But was Liz
really as strong-minded as she thought she was?

THE NIGHT OF THE HURRICANE
by Andrea Blake

Julie's idyllic life on a lonely Caribbean island ended when
her father remarried and her stepmother tried to persuade
him to sell the place. Even after her marriage to Simon
Tiernan, Julie felt her stepmother's malicious influence.

MASK OF SCARS
by Anne Mather

Christina's brother was running a hotel in the Algarve, in
southern Portugal, so when her long vacation came along, it
struck her as a good idea to go and spend it with him. At
any rate, it seemed a good idea until she realised just how
unwelcome she was! Nevertheless, she soon began to wonder
if she had done the right thing when she took the job
offered her by the local lord of the manor . . . .

A MAN OF AFFAIRS
(The Widening Stream)
by Rachel Lindsay

When Melanie Powell became engaged to an American, she
invited her friend Loris Cameron to accompany her on a visit
to his family home in California, and on the way Loris too
fell in love — with Brett Halliday. But both girls were to have
a long way to travel before they reached the end of their
journey to happiness.

Mills & Boon Classic Romances
— all that's best in Romantic Reading

Available November 1979